THE TEXAS BRIGADE

A SHAWN STARBUCK WESTERN

THE TEXAS BRIGADE

RAY HOGAN

*Large Print
Western
Hogan, R,*

THORNDIKE
CHIVERS

This Large Print edition is published by Thorndike Press, Waterville, Maine, USA and by BBC Audiobooks Ltd, Bath, England.

Thorndike Press is an imprint of Thomson Gale, a part of The Thomson Corporation.

Thorndike is a trademark and used herein under license.

The text of this Large Print edition is unabridged.

Other aspects of the book may vary from the original edition.

Set in 16 pt. Plantin.

LIBRARY OF CONGRESS CATALOGING-IN-PUBLICATION DATA

Hogan, Ray, 1908–
  The Texas brigade : a Shawn Starbuck western / by Ray Hogan. — Large print ed.
    p. cm. — (Thorndike Press large print western)
  ISBN-13: 978-0-7862-9555-5 (hardcover : alk. paper)
  ISBN-10: 0-7862-9555-4 (hardcover : alk. paper)
  1. Starbuck, Shawn (Fictitious character) — Fiction. 2. Sheriffs — Fiction.
3. Texas — Fiction. 4. Mexico — Fiction. 5. Kidnapping — Fiction. 6. Large
type books. I. Title.
PS3558.O3473T465 2007
813&prime.54—dc22   2007005600

BRITISH LIBRARY CATALOGUING-IN-PUBLICATION DATA AVAILABLE

Published in 2007 in the U.S. by arrangement with
Golden West Literary Agency.
Published in 2007 in the U.K. by arrangement with
Golden West Literary Agency.

U.K. Hardcover: 978 1 405 64154 8 (Chivers Large Print)
U.K. Softcover: 978 1 405 64155 5 (Camden Large Print)

Printed in the United States of America on permanent paper
10 9 8 7 6 5 4 3 2 1

THE TEXAS BRIGADE

1

Bisbee and its brawling main street, Brewery Gulch, had not been a total loss to him, Starbuck was forced to admit as he rode his big sorrel down the long grade leading into the Mesilla Valley. Seeking his brother, Ben, he'd been in Tombstone, a bristling new town surging to prominence in the San Pedro Hills of Arizona Territory, and having no luck there, had pushed on to that next and not too distant settlement in the Mule Mountains where copper, rather than silver, was king.

One evening, making his inquiries along the town's aptly named saloon and crib-lined thoroughfare, he had encountered a man, a furloughed freight-skinner biding his time until management, hopefully, called him back into service. He'd known a Damon Friend in Mesilla, he said, calling Ben by the alias he affected, and while he'd not been back to the town in over a year, it was his guess Friend was still there, dealing blackjack in a saloon that stood on the east side of the plaza.

It was a slim lead and a cold one, Starbuck realized, but it was all he'd been able to turn up, and at such times even rumor lends encouragement; thus, a few days later, after replenishing his war bag, he headed east for the old, short-lived Confederate Territory capital on the Rio Grande.

This would be either his second or third visit to Mesilla in his quest for Ben, he was not certain which; the names of the towns in which he'd paused, as were the endless, lonely trails and many faces, now only indistinct blurs melting into the days and months of the past years.

It had been and still was a discouraging search, one begun shortly after the death of their father, Hiram, who had decreed in his will that Shawn must first find his wayward brother, wherever he might be, and return him to the family lawyer in Ohio before any settlement of the estate could be made.

Starbuck had been no more than a raw farm boy when he undertook to fulfill his father's wishes, but change had come quickly and the youth soon became a man able to hold his own amid the company in which he chose to move, or that by chance he was compelled to join.

Old Hiram, hard-crusted but fair, had erred, however, in that he had provided no funds with which Shawn could conduct the search for the son who had stormed out of their lives after a minor quarrel; but in so doing, it was likely he had performed an important service for the younger Starbuck, be it unwittingly, since it had forced him to halt periodically during the search that carried him from border to border and replenish his purse by taking whatever employment was available.

In so doing, Shawn's experience with both vocation and men broadened until he was now seasoned in many fields, highly respected for not only his prowess with the worn-handled forty-five he wore strapped low to his left thigh, but as a cool, if hardened, trail rider of unquestioned honesty and reliability.

But he need have no thoughts now of looking for work — at least for some time. A job he'd taken in Tombstone, as shotgun rider on an ore wagon, had brought him two hundred dollars. With such a generous stake, he could carry on for several months.

Reaching the foot of the grade, Starbuck halted, let his glance rest upon the small settlement crouching near the river. The fields still appeared green, and while leaves had long since fallen from the giant cotton-woods that marked the little oasis in a broad world of sand, gray brush, and tan grass, the town yet had a warm and friendly look, despite the late season.

Above it the sky was a clean, unscathed blue, and the pair of eagles soaring and dip-ping lazily against it seemed more to be whiling away time rather than searching the valley below for prey.

Motionless, Starbuck continued to study the land before him. A lean, muscular man with slatelike eyes and dark hair, he ap-peared much older than his twenty-two years, a fact achieved perhaps by the re-moteness of his features and the full mus-tache that now graced his upper lip and over-shadowed his somewhat set mouth. An even six feet in height and a score of pounds short of two hundred, he was one not easily overlooked and usually left to his own devices by others.

Someday — someday he'd have a home of his own, he thought, perhaps live in a fine little town like Mesilla, where all was quiet. He would put behind him all recollections of the endless trails he'd followed and forget the tenseness and flaring violence that too often had been his companions.

He'd own his life then, live it according to his personal wishes, and, if lucky, with a woman who loved him and whom he cared for. There'd be no days ahead then waiting for him to mount up, ride, search and complete the task of searching that had been placed upon him.

Instead he would be looking forward to a family, and to raising cattle and possibly the breeding of good horses. His time and his plans would all be his own, not built upon the thoughts of where next to look for a brother he scarcely knew and only vaguely remembered. That time would come — it had to come, and soon, else, as he'd been warned by many whom he'd encountered during his wanderings, he'd wear away the years and one day awaken to the realization that his life had slipped by — spent in the interests of others.

But he'd had no choice; his sense of obligation not only to old Hiram, but to Ben as well, had dictated his course, and while there had been times in the years past when he had questioned himself and his determination to continue the search, conscience had always won out, and he had pushed aside whatever personal interest had laid claim upon him, and ridden on.

Twisting about on the saddle, he gazed off

into the south, toward Mexico, his mind automatically, as always, beginning to shape plans for the continuation of the hunt should Mesilla prove to be a dead end. It was second nature to him now — the lift of hopeless tingling with each successive and fruitless termination, the dull crush of disappointment, less noticeable and wounding after those first months — to plan beforehand where next he would try.

It had developed into an almost monotonous routine, salvaged from deadlines only by the in-between breaks that came occasionally and called upon him to undertake some side issue that brought his abilities into play and made it all bearable.

He'd ride on to Mexico, he decided, raking the gelding lightly with his spurs and swinging him into a lane that led between two adjacent fields. If there was nothing for him in Mesilla, he might as well try the border towns. Reaching the end of the narrow road, he cut north, drawing abreast of a scatter of small adobe houses and finally broke out into the plaza of the town itself.

A half-a-dozen men lolled in the grassy bandstand area of the square's center. Two women were entering a store on the opposite side, but he gave all little notice, simply veered the sorrel toward the saloon standing on the corner to his right.

Pulling up to the hitchrack, he dismounted, pausing for a moment in the ankle deep dust to let his leg muscles find their ease, and then stepping forward, wound the leathers around the rail, and crossing the porch entered the shadow-filled building.

The low-ceilinged room, a bar across one end, a dozen or so tables and chairs occupying most of its remainder, was deserted except for a balding, round-faced man behind the counter and a cowhand sleeping off a drunk in a back corner. Halting at the bar, Shawn nodded.

"Rye whiskey —"

The barkeep wagged his head indifferently. "Beer and bourbon. Ain't got nothing else — 'cepting tequilla."

"Bourbon'll do," Starbuck said, and reached into his pocket for a coin.

"Two bits," the barman said, pouring a shot glass full of the liquor and taking up the silver dollar.

Starbuck sipped at the liquor, glanced at the three quarters in change slid to him across the counter, raised his eyes to the aproned man.

"Was told you had a blackjack dealer by the name of Damon Friend working here."

"Reckon you was told right — only he ain't around no more."

Starbuck shrugged, nudged one of the quarters toward the man for a refill. . . . The same old story — he was always too late. Probably a year late this time.

"How long's he been gone?"

"About a year now, I reckon. What're you asking about him for? You a lawman?"

"Family business. He's my brother."

The barkeeper studied Shawn quietly as he brimmed the shot glass again. Over in the corner the cowhand snorted, shifted his position.

"You do sort've look like him all right," the saloonman conceded reluctantly. "Guess you're kin."

"Know where I can find him?"

"Maybe. Leastwise, I know where he was headed."

Shawn tossed off the liquor, set the glass on the counter. A year was a long time. Ben could have gone to a dozen different places in that much time — but knowing which direction he'd taken would be of some value.

"Where?"

"Texas. Was scouting for some folks from back east — taking them to a place over in the Pecos River country."

14

"Wagon train?"

"Yeh. Teamed up with them somewheres in Kansas, when the fellow they'd hired quit. Was aiming for California, but when they got here they heard about the Pecos country and changed their minds. Had him switch around and light out for there."

Shawn nodded slowly, picked up his change. He understood now why he'd lost track of Ben — he'd been on the trail with a party of immigrants and far away from the towns where he could have been expected to be — but at least it was some word concerning him.

"How long ago was that?" he asked, idly.

"About ten days ago," the barkeeper said.

2

Starbuck drew up in surprise, his pulse quickening. Ten days! He had somehow gotten the impression the saloonman was speaking in terms of a year ago! Figuring the usual speed of travel enjoyed by a wagon train, the party — and Ben — would be no more than three days away for a man on horseback, two if he pressed his mount.

"How far to where they're going?" he asked.

"Three hundred mile, more or less."

Shawn smiled, glanced toward the door as four men entered, quickly lined up at the bar. He nodded to them absently, a flush of relief and pleasure slipping through him. At long last he was going to catch up with Ben; once or twice before he had come close to overtaking him — and then by accident. This time it was different. He knew approximately where Ben was — and where he undoubtedly would be for several days to come.

"Come on, Jess, let's have some of that rotgut you're passing off on folks for whiskey," he heard one of the newcomers say as the bartender moved down the counter to greet them.

"And don't you go shortcutting them glasses, neither!" another added.

The barman said something under his breath. All four of his customers laughed. Over in the corner the cowhand still slept.

"You pulling out right away after your brother?" Jess asked, returning to where Starbuck, elbows hooked on the edge of the counter, head slung forward, was taking his ease.

"Not 'til morning," Shawn replied. "Now that I know where I can find him, there's no big rush. Horse of mine can use a little rest. Same goes for myself."

The saloonman wiped at the counter with a damp cloth, cast a meaningful look at the men at its opposite end. Starbuck frowned, immediately noting the change in his manner.

"Some reason I ought to move on?"

Jess leaned forward slightly, placing his back to the others. "Bird on the end there — one with the whomper-jaw. Name's Duke Holloway. Got a ranch up the valley a piece."

"So —"

"He had some trouble with your brother."

"What kind?"

"Was before Damon went to work here," Jess said confidentially, resuming his polishing. "He'd blowed into town flat busted. Was hunting a stake so's he could keep moving on. Set up a fight — an exhibition he called it; he's one of them fancy boxer kind of fighters, but I reckon you know that."

Starbuck nodded.

"Offered to take on anybody in a ring. Fight was to be held in old man Jamison's barn and the winner got the whole pot — tickets cost a dollar.

"Holloway, there, he's sort of the big cheese around here. Always figured himself a real stem-winder when it come to scrapping, so right away he jumped at the chance to show folks what a humdinger he really was."

"And got himself whipped to a frazzle —"

"For certain! Never seen a man take such a beating. Your brother offered to stop it a couple of times, 'specially after Holloway's jaw got busted, but old Duke just kept at it. Afterward he claimed he hurt his hand right off the start, otherwise it'd turned out different."

"Any truth to that?"

"Hell, no. Nobody believed it — and Damon was right here all the time if he'd been of a mind to do something about it, because he started working here, dealing cards. Was ready to take on Holloway again if that's what Duke wanted — only he didn't. Sure done a lot of big talking and threatening, but it never got past that. Was a couple of months before your brother rode on, heading east.

"And you think this Duke Holloway maybe'll try working his grudge out on me? Fight was a long time ago, and he doesn't know me —"

"You look enough like Damon for him to see it if he gets up close — and he ain't never forgive him for that lacing he took. Humbled him a plenty before his friends, and I expect that's still burning inside his belly. . . . Now, there's a side door leading into the alley —"

Starbuck shrugged, shook his head. "It's my brother he's got a quarrel with, not me."

"Your business," Jess said, smiling. "Figured you best know about it."

Shawn nodded, laid the two quarters change he'd picked up back on the counter.

"I'm obliged to you for doing so. . . . Like to buy you a drink."

Jess grinned, reached for a glass, and refilling Starbuck's, poured himself a full measure.

"Expect you got to know Ben, you call him Damon, pretty well," Starbuck said, as the barman raised his glass and took a swallow.

"For a fact, I did. Was as good a man as you'll ever come across. Maybe not the best gambler that ever shuffled a deck, but he was honest at it and that's what counts with me. Was a time —"

"Jess — goddammit — how about paying some mind to this here end of the bar?"

The saloonman set down his drink, winked at Shawn, and taking up the bottle before him, moved to where the rancher and his three friends were lounging against the counter. He filled their glasses without comment, took the money shoved at him, and returned to Shawn.

"Judging from the load Duke and them was carrying when they got here, I expect they hit every saloon they come to on the way here from Cruces."

Starbuck considered the group for several moments. "Sometimes a man needs to blow off. Guess this is as good a way as any. . . .

Ben ever talk much about home, about me, maybe?"

Jess poured another round of the somewhat raw bourbon. "Nope, was plenty closemouthed when it come to things like that. There trouble between you?"

"Was him and our pa. Never amounted to anything much — just a sort of difference, a misunderstanding I reckon you could call it. I've been looking for him now for quite a spell, even left word here and there so's he'd know I was trying to get in touch with him."

"This here's a mighty big country, and there's a lot of folks on the move."

"Realize that, but still seems logical he'd hear about me hunting him somewhere along the line and try to get together."

The saloonman stirred, rubbed at his chin. "Maybe this ain't for me to say, but you ever think there's a chance he plain don't want to meet up with you?"

"No reason for him to feel that way. Trouble was between him and Pa."

"Could still be the answer. Maybe he's wanting to sidestep having any words with you about your pa — something like that."

"Pa's dead, so's there's no cause for him to feel that way now. Point is, he left quite a bit of money to the two of us, but it can't be touched until I find Ben, get him back to

21

sign some papers. Once that's done he can hide out from me all he wants — if that's what he's doing."

There was a trace of bitterness in Starbuck's tone, and for a time the saloonkeeper made no comment. Then, "I don't expect it's that way. Just how things happen."

"Maybe, but from what you tell me I'm pretty sure he could use the money."

"Well, sure looks like you're going to meet up with him this time," Jess said, finally. "Ought to catch up with that wagon train in two or three days. Five wagons in the bunch. Headed up by a man named Luddin."

"They move out due east?" Shawn asked, his somber mood changing.

"Nope, can't cut straight across like folks used to do. 'Paches are plenty bad in that part of the Territory. Same goes for Texas. Man has to swing south, go by El Paso and follow the river 'til he gets to Sabine Springs. Then he can cut slanchwise toward the Pecos. Regular trail there. Was made by the army back in '49."

Starbuck nodded. Weariness was at last beginning to overtake him. Smiling, he extended his hand to Jess.

"Obliged to you for all your help. Be heading out early, so chances are I won't see you again. . . . There a hotel close where I can stable my horse and get a bed?"

"Sure — across the plaza. Can eat there, too."

Shawn started to turn. The saloonman said, "You see Damon, say my hellos to him and —"

Starbuck swung his attention to the left. Holloway, friends gathered around him, had drawn his pistol and was staring at him closely.

Jess swore deeply, motioned the rancher back. "No it ain't, Duke. You're looking at another man."

"The hell I am! That's the same jasper that tricked me. I ain't blind!"

"Happens to be Damon's brother. They just look quite a bit alike."

A slow smile spread across Holloway's face. "A brother, eh?" he said, holstering his gun. "Well, now, that's mighty nice!"

The saloon owner started to make a reply. Starbuck raised a hand, waved him to silence, and turned to face the rancher fully. He was tired and his humor was none too good. Under other circumstances he likely would have ignored Duke Holloway, but at that moment he was not inclined to be hassled.

"Whatever you're thinking, mister, you'd

best forget it," he said coldly. "Your problem's between you and my brother. It's got nothing to do with me."

"Now, maybe it has," Holloway said thickly, moving up. He glanced at his friends gathered eagerly about him and grinned. "I got a little message you can give him for me next time you meet up."

The rancher lunged, balled fist swinging wide for Starbuck's jaw. Shawn pulled nimbly aside. His left shot out, caught Holloway on the side of the face; his right buried itself in the man's belly.

Duke Holloway halted abruptly, mouth flared, breath rasping through his slack lips. For a long moment he hung motionless, and then growling an oath, he surged forward again, arms outstretched, spread fingers clawing for Starbuck's throat.

Shawn dipped low, spun, pulled away from the counter. Pivoting again, he came in from the side, arms working like pistons, fists drumming a tattoo on Holloway's body, neck, and head. The rancher staggered and caught himself against the bar to keep from going down. Starbuck, cool as winter's wind, nailed him with a stiff left to the nose that brought a spurt of blood, followed with a sharp right to the ear that pulled Duke half around.

Nearby the men with Holloway stood silent and motionless, not inclined to take a hand in the proceedings which they were watching dully. The sleeping cowboy, aroused by the scuffling, was now on his feet and looking on in heavy-eyed wonderment.

"Back off," Starbuck snarled, as Holloway began to gather himself and draw erect. "You're drunk and I'm damned tired."

"Hell with that," Duke rumbled and lurched forward once again.

Shawn, untouched by the man's wildly swung blows, jerked away, took a short step, wheeled. His knotted fist, traveling full distance, connected squarely with Duke's chin. Holloway came to a sudden full stop. His head snapped back and his eyes rolled whitely. His arms fell limply to his sides as his knees began to quiver.

Starbuck, poised before him, doubled fists ready to deliver more punishment, gave the rancher a brief, searching glance. Sheer will alone was keeping the man from going down. He was out on his feet.

Reaching out, Shawn caught him by the shoulders, and turning him about, shoved him into the arms of his friends.

"Take him home and put him to bed," he snapped, and nodding tautly to Jess, crossed the room to the doorway, and stepped out into the open.

3

He was being trailed. Starbuck discovered that shortly after he rode out of Mesilla early that next morning.

A gust of impatience shook him. After all that time, he was finally going to meet with his brother, and now, with a night's rest behind him, the thought of any delay irked him.

Following along the good road that cut its course southward through groves of thick-trunked cottonwood trees beneath which explorers coming up from Mexico had no doubt camped centuries earlier, he began to angle more toward the low hills to his left. An occasional ragged-face butte could be seen through the brush and unquestionably there would be many gullies and arroyos into which he could turn and wait unseen while those behind him caught up.

A quarter hour later he drew into one such cleavage, and dismounting, tied the gelding to a clump of rabbitbush. Moving quickly, he doubled back to where he had a clear view of the trail.

In a few minutes three riders broke into view. It was who he had expected — Duke Holloway, this time with only two of the men who'd sided him in the saloon. Evidently the third member of his party had found better things to do.

Shawn watched them draw abreast. The rancher's battered face was dark and swollen and his eyes appeared to be almost closed. He rode slightly ahead of the others and there was a rifle resting across his legs. His friends, reluctance showing in their expressions, were staring straight forward.

Delaying while the riders passed, and until he was certain the fourth man was not just lagging behind, Starbuck stepped out into the open.

"Right here, Holloway," he called, "if it's me you're looking for."

Startled, the men pulled up short, wheeled. Duke, trembling with anger, gripped the rifle tightly, started to swing it about, then checked himself, apparently having second thoughts about the wisdom of such a move.

"Come for you, all right," he said through

thick lips after several moments of uncertainty.

"Here I am," Starbuck said flatly. Legs spread, arms hanging at his sides, he faced the rancher. "What've you got on your mind?"

"Yesterday — that's what. I don't let nobody work me over like that and get away with it."

"You want to try your luck again? Happens I'm in a hurry, so if that's what you're thinking, step down and let's get it over with."

Holloway gave that thought, began to swing stiffly off his horse. Shawn swore angrily. He'd hoped the man would back off and ride on. Another brawl could cost him an hour, possibly longer.

"You're mighty tough with a man who's had a few drinks," Holloway said, coming about slowly.

"Was you that picked the time," Shawn snapped and swung his hard glance to the two men still in their saddles. "You cutting yourself in on this?"

Both shook their heads. Starbuck nodded. "Don't make any sudden moves then if you want to stay healthy."

Holloway, still holding the rifle, bucked his head at the weapon on Starbuck's hip.

"You chucking that iron?"

"When I see you put that rifle back in the boot where it belongs and drop your belt —"

"Ain't figuring to," Holloway yelled, and whipped the long-barreled gun into line.

Starbuck dipped forward, drew and fired all in the same breath. He had expected Holloway to pull a trick of some sort and was alert for it.

As the rifle boomed, the report drowning that of the pistol, the rancher rocked back. Dropping his weapon, he clawed at his arm.

"Goddamn you!" he screamed. "You can't —"

Shawn, attention now on the two riders, nodded coolly at them.

"He's not bad hurt, but you sure as hell better get him out of my sight — quick. He tries something like that again on me, I won't be feeling so charitable."

Both men dismounted hurriedly and moved up to the rancher. One picked up the fallen rifle, carefully taking it by the barrel so there would be no mistaking his intentions; the other, sliding an arm around Duke Holloway's middle, turned him toward his horse.

"Come on, boss," he coaxed. "Ain't no sense pushing this no farther."

Holloway muttered a reply and allowed himself to be escorted to his mount. Grabbing the saddle horn with one hand, he looked back. Anger and hate twisted his already distorted face.

"Ain't done with you yet, drifter!" he snarled. "Be another day come and I'll —"

"Smartest thing you can do is forget that," Shawn cut in. "But if you're fool enough to try, I'll be riding through here again sometime."

The rancher ground out a reply, made as if to wheel and resume the encounter, but his two friends turned him back and with some effort got him up onto his horse. Not moving, pistol still in his hand, Shawn watched the others go to the saddle, and then flanking the rancher, head back down the road for Mesilla.

When they rounded the first bend and were lost to sight, Starbuck trotted back to where he'd left the sorrel, and swinging onto the big horse, spurred him onto the trail and resumed his journey at a brisk lope. That damned Holloway had cost him a good half hour.

Some time after noon that next day, when he topped out a low rise just north of the Rio Grande, he saw the town of Sabine

Springs lying in a brown and gray blur in the distance.

Taking the advice of Jess, the Mesilla saloonkeeper, he had veered southward, avoiding the country where Apaches were said to be running wild, and further bypassing El Paso, reached the old Spanish settlement of Ysleta. The Luddin party had passed that way, a stableman in the town had assured him, and the scout leading it was following the established route laid out by the army.

He'd pressed on after resting the sorrel for an hour, keeping to the main trail taken by Ben, rather than angling direct across the desolate, barren land that rolled away from the sluggishly flowing river on both sides.

Undoubtedly he could have saved time and many miles if he chose to take a short cut, but there was always the possibility of trouble. Wheels did break now and then, as did axles, and sickness could bring about a halt. To forsake the exact course being taken by the wagon train, although more circuitous, could cause him to override the party if a delay had occurred.

It was a long, hard ride made only less than tedious by the trees and shrubbery growing along the river and the occasional villages he noted on the Mexican side of the Rio Grande, which served as a boundary between the two countries. Once he was past El Paso, he met only two travelers, both men who seemed in a great hurry to reach their destination.

The sorrel slipped into an easy lope as he moved down the gentle grade for the settlement, while within Starbuck a sort of expectant tension began to build. If he was running in luck, Ben and the Luddin wagon train would still be in Sabine Springs, resting up, as they might be expected to do before undertaking the final leg of their journey to the Pecos country.

It was only a hope, but he couldn't help wishing such would prove to be the case. However, if it turned out otherwise, it wouldn't matter too much; the party couldn't be too far ahead, and in a short time he would be able to overtake them.

He reached the edge of the town — no more than two dozen buildings and homes — and swung onto the main street. Sabine Springs was apparently little more than a midway stop along the route, as there seemed to be little else to support a settlement other than a few small farms lying to the rear of weathered and lonely looking houses.

Evidently it was a time of some importance to the residents, Shawn decided, seeing a fairly large group of people gathered in the center of the business district, but he gave it little thought; the people of Texas were always commemorating one thing or another. He rode on, barely noting the assemblage other than it was centered around a horse and rider and that it was taking place in front of the marshal's office, his eyes searching instead for the wagon train. After a bit he shrugged; there was no sign of the Luddin party — they had already pulled out.

Ignoring the glances turned to him, Starbuck wheeled the sorrel into the hitchrack fronting Benjamin's General Store and dismounted. He was getting low on a few items — coffee, salt, bacon, biscuits, and the like. He'd best rebuild his supply while he had the opportunity.

Securing the gelding, he stepped up onto the landing jutting out from the building and started for the door. A voice from the street halted him.

"You want something?"

Shawn turned, faced a large, red-haired man wearing a stained bib apron. Evidently he was Benjamin, the owner of the place.

"Running short on grub," Starbuck replied, and then, as a sudden clamor of words came from the crowd, he paused and jerked a thumb toward it. "What's going on?"

"The marshal's getting a posse together."

"A holdup or something?"

"Comancheros," the storekeeper said. "Jumped a wagon train that passed through here a few days ago. Kidnapped the whole shebang, took them across the line into Mexico."

Starbuck had come to stiff attention. A coldness was moving through him as he faced Benjamin.

"That wagon train — was the man scouting for them named Friend — Damon Friend?"

The merchant nodded slowly, a frown crossing his face as he studied Shawn. "Yeh, that's what they called him," he said.

4

For a long breath Starbuck was a stiff, unmoving shape in the sunlight. Then he wheeled, stepped down into the dust, and crossed to where the crowd had gathered. Shouldering his way through the men, women, and children, he halted before the rider, an elderly, hollow-cheeked individual with a pocked skin.

"You sure it was Comancheros that hit that wagon train?" he asked tautly.

The man drew up, indignation tightening his features. "Course I'm sure! Reckon I've been around these parts long enough to know what I'm talking about."

"You get a look at them?"

"Nope," the man drawled, "happened two, maybe three days before I come along. Tracks heading off past the Eagle Tails for the border was plenty plain, though. Weren't hard to see what went on."

"There look like there'd been any fighting?"

"If you're meaning do I think anybody got hurt, the answer's no. Comancheros don't hurt nobody they grab. Want to keep them good and healthy so's they'll bring top price when they sell them. . . . Some of them folks kin of —"

"Never mind, Jake," a voice cut in quietly.

Shawn shifted his attention to the speaker, a tall, whiplike man with gray hair and eyes and a craggy face all ridges and furrows. The star he was wearing bore the faded black lettering: MARSHAL.

"Who're you, mister?" he asked.

"Name's Starbuck. If that was the Luddin party, the scout leading it is my brother —"

"Called hisself Friend —"

"Just a name he uses. . . . Was hoping to catch up with them here."

The lawman nodded, extended his hand. "I'm John Mayo, the marshal here. Used to be with the Rangers."

There was a noticeable ring of pride in the lawman's tone. Shawn took his slender, bony fingers into his own, pressed them firmly.

"Pleased to know you. . . . Understand you're mounting a posse —"

"What I'm doing," Mayo said briskly,

glancing about the crowd. "Got eight men recruited, not counting myself. You'll make nine if you're aiming to go after your brother."

"That ain't but ten in all!" Jake, the man who'd brought in word of the attack, exclaimed. "Why, there must've been thirty, maybe forty of them Comancheros, figuring from the tracks."

"You ain't going to be able to do no good with a little dab of men like that," a voice from the crowd said. "Best you send for the army."

"Ten Texans," a second voice observed, "is a mighty powerful bunch of men, once they set their heads to doing something. Every bit as good as a whole brigade!"

Someone laughed, hushed instantly. Starbuck said: "Count me in, but there's probably good sense in getting word to the army."

"Expect to do that, but we can't hold off until they get around to doing something. First thing they'll have to do is get an approval from the Mexican government before a United States soldier can step a foot over the border — and the Lord only knows how long that could take."

"I'll bet old Sam Houston'd not wait!" someone declared.

"Maybe not, but things've changed a mite since he was around. Point is, *we* can't wait. Time the army gets going, Valdez and his bunch'll have sold them folks off as slaves and be long gone somewheres in the Sierra Madres."

"Just what I said — Sam Houston'd not wait — not for nobody!" the same voice insisted. "He'd go right ahead come hell or high water!"

"How about the Mexican army?" Starbuck wondered.

"Ain't no post anywheres close to us," the lawman said. "Them Comancheros have been raising hell all this past summer and they've kept the Federalistas hopping, but with all the ground they've got to cover, I don't think they've had much luck catching them."

"If you ask me, I ain't so sure they're wanting to," a man leaning against the front of the marshal's office said drily. He was elderly also, like Mayo. His ragged beard and trailing mustache were tobacco stained, and the buckskins he was wearing showed many years of hard service. But his eyes were sharp and there was a keenness to his manner. . . . An old army scout, Shawn guessed.

"Hell, Zeb, you can't be sure of that," the

marshal said, frowning.

"Can't prove it, you mean," Zeb snapped. "But you know it, same as me and a lot of us do. Ever since they opened up them new silver mines in the Chihuahua hills, the Comancheros've been running wild, and folks've been dropping out of sight. Was a man able to pay a call on them mines, he'd find a lot of his missing friends and relatives right there swinging a pick and shovel!"

A chorus of agreement went up from the crowd. Mayo wagged his head. "I ain't saying you're wrong, I'm only saying you don't know for sure —"

Starbuck, worry over Ben deepening with the passing minutes, stirred impatiently. It seemed to him time was being wasted in a lot of useless talk and wrangling.

"Marshal, how soon are we pulling out?" he asked, turning to Mayo.

"Coming to that right now," the onetime Ranger said, his tone abruptly all business. "Want every one of you riding with me to be mounted and ready to go in one hour. Meeting place'll be Johnson's barn. We're traveling light, so bring your own grub and water — aim to live off the land much as possible."

"Off the land!" a grinning young cowhand echoed in a scoffing voice. "We're sure going to have mighty slim pickings, Marshal! All we'll find where we're going is Gila monsters, scorpions, and a few rattlesnakes!"

"You just look out for your own belly, Davey Joe," the lawman shot back. "Same goes for every man jack in this outfit — he's got to look out for hisself, Ranger style."

"I got a couple of pack mules you're welcome to use, John," a man somewhere in the back of the gathering suggested.

"Obliged, Henry, but they'd slow us down too much. We'll do our own packing. . . . Anybody else got something to say?"

There was no response. The marshal bobbed his head smartly. "All right then, get at it!"

The crowd began to break up. Mayo stepped in close to Shawn. "Seen you getting a mite fidgety," he said. "You pulling out alone or are you still aiming to come along with us?"

"Riding with you long as we're going after the same bunch —"

"Fair enough. However, you being a stranger here, we best get one thing straight; I'm running this posse. You'll take orders from me."

"Suits me," Starbuck said coolly, and

wheeling, retraced his steps to Benjamin's store.

The merchant was behind a counter in the rear. Slouched against the shelving and arms folded across his chest, he was sourly watching another man with a remarkable likeness to himself, moving about the store, dropping various food items into a flour sack. Shawn had noticed the man among the crowd, a big redhead with a reckless look on his broad face. He was to be one of the posse members, apparently.

Benjamin came erect as Starbuck halted at the counter. "Ready for that grub you're needing?"

Shawn nodded, named off the items on his mental list. From across the room the redhead grinned at him.

"Going to be like old times," he said.

Starbuck smiled, puzzled. Benjamin paused. "He's talking about the army. Rode with Nate Forrest during the war and ain't never got it out of his blood. You going with the posse?"

"About the only way I'll catch up with my brother," he said, and added, "Better throw a box of forty-fives in with the rest of that stuff."

The storekeeper reached back to a shelf for a box of cartridges, pointed with it at the redhead. "My brother, Deke — might as well know each other since you'll be riding together. Your name's Friend, I take it."

Deke had stepped from behind the counter and was offering his hand. Taking it, Shawn said, "No, name's Starbuck."

"I see — half brother —"

Starbuck shrugged. "Fact is he just calls himself that. Real name's Ben." He stopped there, feeling no need to go into any further explanation. "Little surprised to hear you were having Comanchero trouble. Understood Mackenzie put an end to them when he went through here a few years ago."

"Did. Old Jose Montoya and his bunch were the last of them — but now we've got a new gang running loose. Half-breed by the name of Valdez is leading them, so we hear."

"Lot a truth in what Zeb Traxler said out there in the street," Deke Benjamin added, slinging a pair of well-worn army field-glasses over his shoulder. "New silver mines over in the Chihuahua country've been opened up and they're paying big money for laborers. Making Valdez and his kind rich."

"That where the people they kidnap always end up?"

43

"Far as we know — the men, anyway. Girls and younger women wind up in brothels. Older ones, and kids, probably turn out to be slaves in the rancherias."

"And the Mexican government won't do anything about it?"

"Ain't so far," the storekeeper said, dropping Starbuck's purchases into a sack. "Not saying they don't try —"

"Zeb's right there, too," Deke cut in. He had completed his selection of supplies and was tying a bit of cord about the neck of the container. "They don't want to do something about it. They're getting plenty of taxes out of it, besides the cut they're taking on the side."

Benjamin wagged his head. "Zeb Traxler just ain't got no use for Mexicans. He don't know for sure what he says is the truth. . . . Mines are supposed to be using only convict labor."

"Hell, they say the convicts are worse'n none at all! Most of them are too weak to do a day's work. What them mine people want are the big, strong gringos — and they're getting them, thanks to the damned Comancheros."

"Then there's been other wagon trains?"

"Your brother's outfit's the only one they've grabbed around here," Benjamin

44

said. "We've heard of a couple of others dropping out of sight down around Van Horn's Wells."

"Just ain't no way of telling how many pilgrims they've snatched up — cowhands, men riding across country, peddlers and drummers — gents like that," Deke said. "You ready to go?"

Shawn reached into a pocket, handed a gold eagle to Benjamin. "Soon as I pay off your brother."

"You're paying off both of us," Deke said with a broad wink. "We're partners."

"With me doing all the goddamn work and you horsing around all the time," Benjamin said icily.

"You could lock up this dump and come along," Deke said. "Do you good."

"One fool in the family's a plenty," Benjamin said, returning a handful of change to Shawn. He looked closely at his brother, probably several years younger than himself. "Take care, hear?"

Deke grinned. "Don't I always? You just keep a lamp burning in the window. I'll be back."

Hanging his sack of supplies over a shoulder, the redhead started for the door, paused, swung his attention to Shawn.

"You know where we're meeting?"

"Johnson's barn, wherever that is."

"Edge of town. Might as well go there together, unless you got something else you aim to do."

"Fill my canteen, that's all."

"Can do that at Johnson's. Best we pick us up some grain for the horses there, too. Ain't much forage where we're going."

Starbuck nodded, moved off after the redhead. From the back of the store Benjamin called: "Good luck."

Shawn turned, a wry smile on his lips. "I'm beginning to think we'll need it," he said, and continued on his way.

5

When Starbuck and the redhead arrived, only town Marshal John Mayo and Zeb Traxler, who, according to Deke, would be coming along to do whatever tracking might be necessary, were at the designated starting point. The lawman, clearly now himself impatient, greeted them scowlingly as they rode up to the horse trough and dismounted.

"I'm mighty proud some folks knows I'm in a hurry," he said.

Shawn made no reply. Unhooking his canteen, he removed the cap and poured out what yet remained in it preparatory to refilling it with fresh water.

Traxler said, "They'll be coming, Captain, just keep your shirt on. Some of them's got families they're saying good-bye to — maybe for good."

"Know that, but we already wasted plenty of time. Come dark, I aim to get to the river and be set to ford. As soon nobody'd see us doing that."

"We camping in the hills to the south of there?"

"What I was figuring on," Mayo replied, watching Deke Benjamin approaching from the interior of Johnson's barn. Waiting until the redhead was near, he added, "What you got there?"

"Oats. Me and Starbuck plan on keeping our horses in good shape. Campaign ahead's going to be hard on them."

Mayo swore. "Campaign! You listen to me, Deke, this ain't no army expedition — so don't go making out like it is!"

"You're setting it up like we was a bunch of Rangers —"

"Anything wrong with that?"

"No, only it ain't no more that than it is the army. Probably be better off if we did handle it like old Nate Forrest would. He knew how to get things done."

"And the Texas Rangers didn't — that what you're saying?"

"Nope, ain't saying nothing of the kind. Only —"

Starbuck, canteen filled, secured the cap and hung the container on his saddle. If this was a sample of how the posse would be operating in the days to come, he had grave doubts as to the results. It might be better if he rode on alone, attempted to rescue Ben and the Luddin party on his own.

He gave that possibility consideration, and dismissed it. The odds would be overwhelming, and he would be in country totally unfamiliar to him; such efforts could end not only in disaster for himself but for Ben and the wagon-train party as well.

Picking up the portion of the grain Deke had left for him he stuffed it into his saddlebags, glanced at Zeb Traxler. The old scout smiled faintly, shrugged as if the bickering between the marshal and Benjamin was nothing unusual and to be expected.

Other members of the posse were now beginning to put in their appearance — the brash, young cowhand they called Davey Joe, another boy probably about the same age. Both were riding small chunky horses, and besides a pistol and rifle, each had a long-bladed knife hanging from his belt.

"Aim to carve me up a few Mexes," Davey Joe declared, patting the blade. "My pa used this here Bowie when he was fighting them. I figure it's about time it tasted some blood again."

"Same here," the other boy said. "I'm just honing to whet this here toad-stabber of mine on some Comanchero throats."

Zeb Traxler brushed at his mustache, glared at the pair. "Best you young whelps get one thing in your heads right now," he said, splattering a rock near the water trough with tobacco juice, "them Comancheros ain't nothing like calves about to be throwed! Won't be no funnin' to it. If it's needful, they'll kill you quicker'n you can say Jack Robinson!"

"Don't worry, they ain't going to catch me napping," Davey Joe said.

Deke Benjamin scrubbed at his chin. "Might be a good idea if we left you two behind," he said. "Rest of us'll be too dang busy to be watching out for you."

"Ain't nobody going to have to do that for me!" Davey Joe shouted angrily. "Can take care of myself."

"You just think you can, boy. Going to be four, maybe five of them to one of us."

"That don't mean nothing! Look what the odds were there at the Alamo. Was just a handful of Texans and they stood off the whole Mexican army!"

"Was a fine bunch of mighty brave men, sure enough," Zeb Traxler said. "Too bad they ended up dead."

"Ain't nothing wrong with that —"

"No, reckon not if there's a good reason."

"Well, far as I'm concerned, this here can be another Alamo," Davey Joe said. "I ain't afraid to die if I have to. Ain't that how you feel, Orvy?"

The young man with him nodded somewhat glumly. "Yeh, reckon so."

"Mite different with me," the old scout said. "I ain't in no hurry to cash in my chips, but if the good Lord says it's time, then I expect I will."

"You all listen to what I tell you and it won't come down to dying," John Mayo said, glancing up at two more men riding in. "This ain't going to be no war — no all-out slam-bang of an attack like we was the army. We'll be slipping in quiet and easy, 'Pache style, once we catch up to them, and do our fighting a dab at a time. We'd be blamed fools was we to try and take them straight on."

"Wouldn't be no big chore for us if we could get them hemmed-up in a pocket somewheres —"

The lawman shook his head. "They ain't liable to let us do that, not being pure dumb. . . . You best start understanding what we're up against, boy! Them Comancheros ain't just a bunch of raggedy-ass field hands — they're a mean lot of real tough hombres and just as smart as us."

51

Shawn, sitting on the edge of the water trough, made a count of the men present . . . two short of the expected number. All were still-faced and quiet, preferring to listen to the talkative Davey Joe and the remarks directed to him by Mayo and Traxler, rather than take part. It could be, he decided, that now, with the first flush of heroics over they were realizing the seriousness of the undertaking.

"Where we picking up their trail?" It was Deke Benjamin.

The marshal waved indefinitely toward a low-lying range of hills to the south. "This side of the Eagle Tails. Crossed the river right around there, somewheres, according to Jake Ballew. Won't be no sweat. Wagon wheel tracks ain't hard to follow."

"They got all five of the wagons?"

"Only two. Burned the others. Means they won't be traveling fast. Got all them folks, and whatever goods they fancied, loaded into just two wagons. Having to drive all that extra livestock, too."

"Mighty big start on us, just the same," Traxler grumbled. "And once they get down there along them hills they call the Fierros, they won't be easy to spot."

"That's where you come in," Mayo said. "Be up to you to track them." He turned, looked toward the settlement. "Where the hell's Dagget and Finch? They're holding us up."

"I'll go find them, Captain," Orvy volunteered.

"You stay put," the lawman snapped. "Don't want to have to chase you down, too. . . . I reckon that's them coming now."

Starbuck rose, moved to the sorrel and swung onto the saddle. Finally they were about to get started. He glanced at the sun. He didn't know how far it was to the ford on the Rio Grande, but there were now only a couple of hours left before dark.

"Took your time getting here!" Mayo barked, as the two riders pulled up to the trough.

"Come soon as I could," the older of the pair said, indifferently. "Ain't every day a man pulls up and leaves his business to go chasing after outlaws. Had to make some arrangements."

The marshal scowled, touched each man with his eyes. "Going to do some checking. Once we get moving, ain't nobody turning back for nothing. That clear?"

There was no response.

"All right, then. When I name off, I want you to take a look, see for certain you've got what I'm mentioning. First — grub."

The riders, with the exception of Benjamin, made their investigations and nodded. Mayo glared at the redhead.

"Well, you looking or ain't you?"

"Got my grub sack, don't you worry," Deke said, and dropped his hand on the flour sack hanging from his saddle.

"Extra ammunition — cartridges —"

There was a moment's delay and then again a murmur of assent. Mayo went the entire route: canteen, blanket, weapons, and finished up with, "Whiskey?"

There were three bottles among the party. The marshal's face hardened.

"You know I don't favor drinking — specially on a deal like this, but I ain't denying either that there's times when a swallow or two's necessary.

"Now you hear me good. You keep them bottles in your saddlebags while we're riding. First man I see nipping when it ain't needful is going to find me pouring his whiskey on the ground."

Mayo allowed that to sink in. Then, "Reckon we're set to go unless some of you's got something to say."

There was no answer. The old Ranger lifted a hand, made a sweeping forward motion with it.

"All right, move out!" he shouted.

"In two's."

Starbuck cut the sorrel about, heaved a long sigh. At last they were on the way.

6

They had been in the saddle for little more than an hour when John Mayo began to feel the weight of his years creeping through him again. He shifted angrily, overrode the dull pain with a curse. If it was the last thing he ever did he'd stand it, keep the others from knowing about the hell he was going through.

And this little sashay could very well be just that, he thought grimly. He was a damned-fool jackass to be fooling himself; no matter how hard he tried, or what he said or did, he couldn't turn back the clock and make things like they were thirty or forty years ago.

Unconsciously Mayo straightened a bit on his saddle as a quick recollection of those days flicked through his mind. He'd been high up in the Rangers in his prime years, a tough, straight-down-the-middle lawman respected by his fellow officers as well as other men who wore a badge — and feared plenty by outlaws. Nobody ever gave him any back talk and his judgment was considered faultless.

He'd been in on the capture or killing of two dozen or so of the worst sort of hard cases and the governor himself had once called him in for a commendation. For a time, when Texas folks thought of the Rangers, they thought of John Mayo; he'd been that good, and while he was not the sort to admit it openly himself, he knew it to be a fact.

But then the one thing no man, regardless of his abilities, can overcome — advancing age — began to catch up with him. He found himself becoming slower, growing hesitant and occasionally not certain of his course. A prisoner got away from him, doing it in such easy fashion that it made him look a fool. Later, when he had time to mull it over, he realized that years earlier it wouldn't have happened; he would have simply drawn his pistol and shot the man dead before he'd taken three strides.

Understanding what had occurred to him had been difficult; just what was it that slowed his thought process and stayed his hand? He had thrashed that about in his mind endlessly, and then when it took place a second time, a superior laid it out in cold, cruel words for him; he had simply grown too old for the Rangers. He had a fine record, an enviable one, in fact, but they would have to fill his saddle with a younger man.

John Mayo had retired with all the grace and dignity expected of a hero, and for a year had lain about, taking it easy, basking in the glow of the reputation he had built, still prominent in the minds of the people in his home area.

But the days eventually began to drag, and when he got word that a small town close to the Mexican border was looking for an experienced town marshal, he packed up his gear and rode out.

It had been a pleasant surprise. The citizens of Sabine Springs had welcomed him with open arms. Many of them remembered him from the past, and the idea of hiring on a famed member of the invincible Rangers as their lawman was a stroke of luck none had dared dream of.

He had moved into his quarters and taken over the office at once, again warming to the fires of admiration turned upon him, enjoying fully the open-mouthed stares of young boys engulfed in hero worship. After he'd hung his citations on the walls, along with a framed letter from the governor, and a square of thin board upon which was pasted several newspaper accounts of his more daring exploits, he held a sort of get-acquainted, hand-shaker day and invited the whole country to drop in.

Folks readily accepted his invitation, responding in twos, threes, and larger groups. The schoolmarm even declared an afternoon holiday for the occasion and dropped by with her entire enrollment.

Thus it had started well. He'd had little serious crime to contend with — an occasional drunk, a few thefts, some tax-collection problems, and that about covered it, at least until Valdez and his pack of Comancheros showed up on the scene.

The bandits had marauded pretty well throughout the country around Sabine Springs, burning and looting homesteads, stealing cattle and horses, and occasionally there were reports of the kidnapping of cowhands and travelers caught between points. Strangely, Valdez and his riders seemed to carefully avoid the old Ranger's domain, and it was as if they had no desire to tangle with a lawman of his stature.

It pleased John Mayo to believe that and he held his head a bit higher as he walked about the town where after — Great God, it was now twenty years! — he had long since settled into the routine of being the marshal.

The vicissitudes of life in Sabine Springs were such that a whole new generation now moved about him; the settlement had grown, flourished briefly, and faltered. Many of those who had known him and his reputation well were gone, dead, or migrated to a more promising or comfortable area.

The gaping, worshiping youngsters were now adults, and the ones born subsequent to his advent, such as Davey Joe Harrison and Orville Clark, and who had incidentally missed the importance of having a top grade lawman as their town marshal, were now boys on the verge of manhood.

He had smarted under the stealthy, gray cloak of oblivion that had settled over him, and the sly remarks and covert glances accorded him by many of the townspeople had cut deeply into his pride. He was an old man, he'd heard it said, long past his prime. He'd had his day, but they reckoned he'd do as well as any, since all he had to look out for were Saturday-night drunks and chicken-stealing drifters, but if ever came the time when the town was up against a serious problem, they'd best send for the Rangers.

The Rangers! By hell, maybe they'd forgotten it, or possibly they didn't know, but they had one of the top men in the service wearing their lousy town-marshal star! And if the day ever did come when a strong hand was needed, he'd wake them up to the fact.

And come it had.

First it had been a freighter on the road near Sierra Blanca. The Commancheros had grabbed him and his wagons loaded with goods for El Paso, driven it, wagons, teamsters, horses, and contents across the line into Mexico. Sierra Blanca was out of his territory, but he felt obligated to throw in with the sheriff of that country on the investigation and had learned two things — that it had been Valdez, the half-breed, leading the bunch, and that setting a saddle for any length of time was sheer agony.

The old bullet wounds in his legs and thigh were like abscessed teeth, and the muscles of his back — hell amighty, he didn't realize it was possible to ache so bad until he'd started riding a horse again.

But that was a problem strictly his own, one kept to himself and that, hopefully, would gradually disappear once he got accustomed to a saddle once more.

He had scarcely returned from the trip to Sierra Blanca when the outlaws struck again, this time making off with the Luddin wagon train. Immediately several of the townspeople suggested word be dispatched to Ranger headquarters requesting help. Others insisted that it was army business, since it involved Mexico, and that the request be sent to Fort Bliss.

The flat-out ignoring of him and his authority, plus the insulting question that help be called in, had hit Mayo with all the force of a cannon's blast, and for the first time he had concrete evidence of what he had known deep in his mind but had refused to admit; he was no longer considered capable of enforcing the law; he was a tolerated, pitied old has-been riding a pension job.

The hell he was!

Some of the old fires banked years ago had burst suddenly into flame as he listened to what was being said when word of the wagon train's fate was brought into town. He smiled faintly now as he recalled the looks on the faces of the townspeople when he spoke up, ruling out the suggestion that aid be sent for.

"I'll do no such a damned thing!" he'd snarled. "Happens it's my job and I intend to do it. I'm calling for a posse. We'll move out after that bunch soon as we can get organized."

Someone in the gathering, he wasn't certain now just who it was, had said: "You figure you're up to it, Marshal?"

"Can bet your life on it," he'd answered.

He was betting his *own* life on it, John Mayo now realized. If he failed he was finished, through — completely and forever. But if he succeeded, it would be like old times again. He would have proven the old saw — *once a Ranger always a Ranger,* and folks in Sabine Springs, along with the rest of the country, would start looking up to him and feeling toward him like people did twenty years ago and more.

Riding a bit to the side of the ragged column, Mayo shifted carefully on his saddle to ease his pains as much as possible, and considered the members of his posse.

He could have done a hell of a lot better, but, when you don't have much choice, a man takes what he can get. Davey Joe and Orvy for instance; a couple of big, overgrown boys hardly dry behind the ears, and all busting out to get into a fight. He'd be lucky if he didn't lose the both of them in the first encounter.

Adam Finch, the livery stable owner. Up in his late forties, probably, and a quiet, dark sort of man. He never talked much and kept to himself around town. It was said there was something in his past that bothered him.

Riding beside him was Jed Willard. Jed had once owned a good homestead up in the Trinity River country. A party of renegade Kiowas had slipped in one day while he was working the lower sections of his land, killed his wife and three children. It had broken him, turned him into a drunk.

Mayo had small patience with drunks, whatever their reason for being such, and had made that attitude known. He'd been told that he should be a bit more compassionate, but that was something he took no stock in; either a man was strong enough to take what luck dealt him, or he wasn't, and for the latter he had nothing but scorn.

And then there was Deke Benjamin, who'd never got over being in the army. Still fancied himself an officer in the Confederate cavalry and went around telling everybody who'd listen about all the big things he'd done during the war. All blow, most likely, and there'd be damn little show when the cards were turned up.

Mort Dagget . . . all he had to say for the years behind him was that he was a good hand at driving a stagecoach and riding shotgun. Evidently he wasn't *too* good because the Overland people had let him go, and he'd now been looking for a job for better than a year. If he was as good a man as he claimed, it was damned funny some of the other stage lines hadn't signed him on. . . . In an all out fight with Valdez and his cutthroats he'd probably prove to be of no use.

Zeb Traxler. When it came to tracking, like as not, he was as good as you could find, but Zeb was old and there wasn't much steam left in him — *older than me,* Mayo thought. But Zeb would fight when and if it came down to it and he could be depended upon to give an accounting of himself.

That left only the two strangers, the sullen looking hard case who said his name was Jim Kane and the one claiming to be the brother of the wagon-train scout; Starbuck, he'd said he was called.

Mayo's practiced eye had considered them both coolly, pegged them for a pair of gunslingers and probably wanted by the law. Ordinarily he'd have no truck with their sort, but at a time like this — leading a bunch of stove-up has-beens and two kids, they were just what he needed.

He'd been up against their kind plenty in

the old days, particularly the ones like Kane; he wasn't too sure he had Starbuck figured exactly yet, but it didn't matter. He was glad they were along, and while chances were they'd be hard to handle and maybe balk at his calling the shots, he'd set them down hard if they got out of line, just as he had Deke Benjamin.

Nobody was running this show but himself. It was going to be his party all the way, and it would be he who got the credit for its success — if it was successful. *If.* . . . John Mayo's seamy face tightened. It had to be. This was the last roll of the dice for him.

7

They were moving slowly — too slowly. Starbuck, glancing at the lowering sun, swore silently, impatiently, while they plodded stolidly along; the fear of what could be happening to Ben in the hands of the Comancheros was plaguing his mind relentlessly.

He had a brief impulse to spur forward, draw up beside Mayo — Captain, everyone called him — and make a strong suggestion that they speed up the pace. He brushed the thought aside; the old lawman probably knew what he was doing.

They rode on. The men, other than Davey Joe and Orvy, maintained a somber silence. The two boys, however, kept up a running conversation, laughing and joking back and forth, now and then acting out some thought they had that pertained to the future. Several times the marshal favored them with scowling disapproval, but they paid no heed.

Around an hour before dark, Zeb Traxler, ranging ahead of the party, picked up the tracks of the Comancheros and their captives. Two heavily loaded wagons and about fifty horses, he reckoned, all moving straight across the flats for the Rio Grande.

"Means there's more of them cutthroats than Jake figured," Adam Finch said morosely. "I'm beginning to think we'd a been smart to leave it to the army."

"Some of them horses are wagon-train stock," Traxler pointed out. "Maybe fifteen or twenty of them. Valdez has probably got thirty or so men with him."

"What difference it make how many there are?" Davey Joe demanded. "Ten or a hundred — all the same to me."

No one commented, simply ignored the rash statement. Mayo, looking down at the scout from his saddle, pulled off his wide-brimmed hat, brushed at his graying thatch.

"You tell how old them tracks are?"

Traxler hawked, spat. "Well, was I to guess, I'd say a week."

The lawman nodded thoughtfully. "Means they're maybe a hundred miles ahead of us."

"Depends," Zeb said, climbing back onto his horse. "Country on the yonder side of the river's plenty rough. They ain't going to be making no fast time — not with them wagons weighted down like they are and all that loose livestock to look after."

"Seventy-five miles, then?"

"Sounds more like it to me. We push right smart, could catch up for a look-see at them by tomorrow sundown, maybe."

Mayo frowned. "Ain't so sure of that," he said, abruptly contentious. "We've got to go slow, just to save the horses."

"Why?" Deke Benjamin asked immediately. "Catching up quick's what we're trying to do, ain't it? Horses can do their resting after we've found that bunch."

Starbuck agreed with the redhead, saw several of the other posse members nod assent, but John Mayo was adamant.

"You all best leave the figuring to me," he said coldly, and raising a hand gave the signal to move on.

Shawn felt the glance of the rider alongside him and swung his attention to the man. When earlier they had introduced themselves to each other, he said his name was Jim Kane. Kane was a hard-jawed, pale-eyed individual with a stilled look and a somewhat insolent manner. He wore two bone-handled pistols in cross-belted style.

"You figure that old range bull knows

what he's up to?"

Starbuck grinned slightly. "Reckon we'll find out soon enough."

"Ain't never going to get around to it at this rate."

"Tomorrow ought to be different. He's probably feeling his way and getting strung out. . . . You know this country?"

Kane shook his head. "Nope, was just passing through when I come on to this ruckus. Heard you say you were looking for your brother."

"He was the scout for the wagon train the Comancheros grabbed."

Kane was silent for a long minute. Then, "Expect you know chances for finding him and all the rest of them folks is plenty slim. We're on a mighty cold trail."

"And getting colder. Unless Mayo whips it up a bit tomorrow, I'll be thinking about pushing on alone."

Kane swept the men ahead of them with a deprecating glance. His slumped shoulders stirred. "Likely do as well by yourself as with them counter-jumpers and sodbusters. . . . There's the river."

Shawn looked beyond the column. The Rio Grande appeared to be a ribbon of copper in the setting sun.

"Mayo aiming to cross right away?" Kane

wondered as they slowly approached the water.

"Said something about waiting for dark. Afraid the Federalistas might spot us."

Kane smiled, a tight-lipped sort of grimace devoid of humor. "Seems he knew what he was doing, at that. Got us here at just the right time."

A hundred paces short of the river the lawman called a halt, and saying nothing in the way of explanation, simply waited out the darkening minutes until night had at last settled over the land. Then, again with a hand signal, he moved forward, rode down into a break in the low bank, and out into the stream.

It was evidently a regular fording place as the footing was solid and the water shallow. Reaching the opposite shore without incident, they climbed out, gained a low rise. Not halting, they began to angle toward a line of dark hills to the southeast.

"Be pitching camp there," Mayo said, finally, pointing at the formation. "Now, I don't want no loud talking or laughing and acting the fool. We ain't welcome here and a man never knows for certain where a troop of them Federalistas might be."

"How about the tracks of the wagon?" Finch asked. "Going to be losing them taking off like this."

"Ain't likely," Traxler drawled. "Be my guess they camped there, too. Turns out they didn't, why in the morning I'll start back-tracking 'til I pick them up again."

"If Valdez was planning on selling the men to the mines, seems he'd be moving west," the man named Mort Dagget said. "What makes you think he'd head this way — it's the wrong direction?"

"I know that," John Mayo said testily. "Them mines are west of here, in the Chihuahuas, but he won't go there first off. He'll take them people to his rancheria. There he can sort them out and divvy up the goods they've got.

"Then he'll load up the men and line out for the mines. Could be he might even wait on that, go do some dickering first. They're long on dickering, always out to get the best price they can for what they're selling."

"For my money," Deke Benjamin said tersely, "we'd be smart to keep right on going. Dark like these nights are, we could spot their camp fire a mile off."

"Valdez ain't that kind of a fool," Traxler replied. "He's got to be watching out for them Federalistas, too. He'll be hiding his camp, and the way this country is, it'd be like looking for a three-legged bee in a hive."

"Too bad there ain't a moon," Davey Joe commented. "Could keep right on tracking them."

"Best you be real glad there ain't," Mayo said bluntly, coming into the conversation. "Being dark'll make it a lot easier for us to do what we have to when the time comes. . . . We'll pull up there by them buttes for the night. Aim on moving out at first light."

Starbuck heard Jim Kane laugh quietly. He glanced at the rider, a dim figure silhouetted against the blackness.

"Ain't nobody going to tell the captain nothing."

Shawn grinned. "No doubt about that. Right or wrong, he's going to do it his way."

"Which ain't mine. Was it me calling the tune we'd keep moving while it's dark and nobody could spot us. Valdez and his bunch is bound to be around here somewheres — and finding them quick is worth gambling on. Anyways, if we missed them, we could all spread out and hunt up the wagon tracks.

"But there ain't no use talking to him about it. He's done got his mind set, and with the odds the size they are, a man'd be a damned fool to take out on his own after them bastards."

"For sure," Starbuck replied, "but that's

what I might be doing. Haven't decided yet."

Kane was silent for a long breath. Then, "Well, I always was a fool when it come to bucking odds. If you make up your mind to forget this outfit and go hunting for your brother on your own, say the word. I'll be pleasured to side you."

"Obliged to you," Shawn said quietly. "Tomorrow I'll know."

Jim Kane and Starbuck, teaming for a less than frugal meal, stared into the graying coals of the small fire they had built and then quickly extinguished at Mayo's orders when the coffee was done. Kane thought to himself how much alike they were.

He supposed that accounted for his breaking from his usual pattern and taking to the big rider at their first meeting. Both had ridden the endless trails, seen the elephant, and were being driven relentlessly on by conditions over which they had little, if any, control.

But there was a difference, nevertheless. Starbuck hunted for a long-missing brother; he searched for a haven from himself and what he had unwittingly become. Miles City, Deadwood, Abilene, Fort Worth, Hays, Dodge City, Wichita — a half-a-hundred others, he'd tested them all, and ridden out — like as not with a lawman's posse or a committee of vigilantes dogging his tracks.

Kane was never fully certain how things got started in those places where such departure had been the case; a hard word said in haste, dispute over a pretty woman with a small waist and high breasts, an ace that mysteriously appeared during a game of cards; but it always ended the same — with him holding a smoking forty-five in each hand and backing toward a door to hurriedly mount his horse and leave the town by the shortest route.

It was never anything he actually sought; it just happened. As some men were prone to accidents, he was subject to violence and trouble, and he got out of such by the best and only means at his disposal — an assist from the six-guns he wore around his middle.

As a result, wanted dodgers graced the walls of lawmen's offices scattered across the land, all declaring him a ruthless killer, a calculating, cold-blooded gunslinger, a desperate criminal upon whose head generous rewards had been heaped. . . . That undoubtedly was why he was forever on the move, although he never thought of it in just that light; to him he was simply a man seeking refuge from an insensitive fate that had unaccountably decreed he become what he had become.

He had thought to find that needed shelter in the small, out-of-the-way settlement of Sabine Springs. It was a nothing, a zero in a broad country of important towns and busy cities. There he could settle down, perhaps open a gun shop or a saddlery — things he knew much about — and live out the rest of his life unmolested by either the law or a destiny that so far refused to look the other way and thereby grant him rest and peace.

Kane had found it no different in the little, dried-up wide place along the Texas-Mexican border. He had been there less than a day when the siren call came — trouble in the form of rapacious Comancheros, and unable to resist, had volunteered to become a member of the posse that was to pursue the outlaws.

He should have kept out of it, remained silent, taken no hand in the incident, but the lure of danger and the promise of excitement had been too strong, and with the smell of powder smoke already in his nostrils, he had overridden all sensible objections.

Here he was hunkered by a dead fire sipping hot coffee to ward off the chill of a

Chihuahua Desert night, and, oddly enough, lined up on the side of the law this time, with nine other men only one of whom he figured was worth riding the river with. . . . He hoped Starbuck would decide to pull out in the morning, go looking for his brother on his own; that sure as hell was the way he'd do it.

8

Zeb Traxler had no difficulty that next morning in locating the trail left by the Comancheros and their captives. They had made their night stop in a short canyon a mile or so below where the posse had halted. Long before the sun had broken the eastern horizon Starbuck and the others were on the move.

Mayo now seemed willing to move in haste, and for the first hours of the morning the riders kept their horses to a fair, ground-covering lope across the broad, near-barren flats of the Chihuahua Desert.

It was a desolate land of slashed arroyos, low foothills, sandy mesas, ragged bluffs, their surfaces sparsely covered by cactus, creosote and saltbush, and the like. Here and there an ocotillo, its slender limbs like scarlet tipped wands, stirred gently in the faint breeze; occasionally they passed by a small forest of giant yucca, their stiff, needle-sharp bayonets pointed upward, offering convenient meat hooks for the butcher-birds and nesting sanctuaries for doves.

The night had been cold, with the air clean and dry as gunpowder, but now as midday gradually approached, the sun warmed steadily and soon was making itself felt.

Noon came and John Mayo called a halt to rest the horses and snack briefly on whatever food each man had handy and that did not require cooking. Within an hour he had the posse in the saddle again, and once more following the wagon tracks leading into the southwest.

Starbuck, riding alongside Jim Kane as before, had altered somewhat his opinion of the old lawman. Mayo now showed an anxiety to overtake the outlaw band, and brooked no delays. He was clearly determined to effect a rescue of the Luddin party as quickly as possible. But as daylight gradually faded into darkness in the vast, bleak country, and they saw no signs of the Comancheros, his intensity decreased and disappointment became apparent.

"Tomorrow'll do it," Zeb Traxler reassured him and the others as, later that night, they sprawled around a small fire.

" 'Bout noon, I reckon."

Starbuck noted that the signs of the party's passage were much fresher, and once more he felt the urge to push on and attempt to free Ben and the others on his own. But common sense now put aside the blind urgency to ignore all other factors and undertake the rescue alone; he would only waste himself — and Jim Kane as well, if he insisted on going along. And their absence would weaken the posse to the point where it would surely fail.

It would be no easy task for them at best. Ten men against a large band of desperate outlaws, estimated to be anywhere from thirty to fifty in number. How Captain Mayo planned to pull it off he could only wonder, but the old ex-Ranger lawman undoubtedly had a scheme.

Lying there in the coolness of the dark, the flickering yellow flames of a carefully shielded fire mirroring on the slack faces of the men, Shawn listened idly to the run of talk making the rounds. One of the party had produced his bottle of whiskey, and with Mayo's curtly expressed approval, was handing it about the circle. Starbuck accepted the bottle, helped himself to a warming swallow of its rapidly diminishing contents, and passed it on.

Across the flare, Davey Joe was regaling Orvy Clark with an accounting of an affair he'd had with some girl. Deke Benjamin fingered the pistol he carried, testing its action, rubbing the metal parts with a bandanna. Traxler, long-bladed skinning knife in his right hand, was honing the steel methodically upon a whetstone, the metal flashing brightly and then gone dull as he alternately turned each side to the light. Finch was in low conversation with Jed Willard, while Dagget appeared to be dozing, as were Kane and John Mayo.

Somehow Shawn Starbuck didn't feel at ease in the party. A loner who ordinarily moved pretty much on his own, he was a man who took little satisfaction in numbers; but in this instance he had come to realize that only by the combined efforts of several could purpose be achieved.

Off in a brushy arroyo, a distance to their left, a fox barked sharply. At once Mayo roused, drew himself to a sitting position. Head cocked, he listened into the night. The dry grating of Traxler's whetting had ceased abruptly with the sound as he, too, turned his attention toward it.

"Indians?" Benjamin asked quietly.

The old scout wagged his head. "Ain't no telling for certain. . . . Maybe some of them

Comancheros."

Mayo relaxed slowly. "Expect it was a fox."

Starbuck, at the edge of the fire's glow rolled silently back into the full dark. "Only one way to know," he murmured. "Rest of you stay where you are."

A half-a-dozen strides from the camp he got to his feet, and hunched low, made a quick circle to the wash. Coming up on it from the side, he drew his pistol, eased in carefully, halted. He could hear nothing and see but little in the brushy blackness. After a few minutes he doubled back, moved in on the arroyo from above. Visibility was slightly improved from that angle, but again his careful search turned up nothing — no horses waiting anywhere nearby for certain — and giving it up, he returned to camp.

"Starbuck," he called out softly when he drew close, warning the others of his approach.

"That what it was — a fox?" Traxler asked as he resumed his place by the fire.

"No sign of anything else," Shawn replied.

The scout began to strop his knife once more. "Well, I reckon if it was Indians or Comancheros they'll be back afore sunup."

"Just to be on the safe side," Benjamin said, "I think we'd best stand watch 'til daylight. No sense taking chances. . . . Be an hour a piece. I'll take the first stint."

"Never mind," John Mayo said coldly. "I'll take it."

The balance of the night passed without incident. Shortly after sunrise they were again on the move, the prints of the wagon wheels and accompanying horses still an easily read trail bearing toward a distant range of mountains.

"Expect that's where we'll find them," Traxler said. "Somewheres in them hills."

"Covers a lot of ground," Mort Dagget commented. "I'll bet it's ten miles across them ridges."

"We'll be depending on the trail they left," Mayo said. "Hell, you don't think I'm figuring to start looking into every one of them canyons do you?"

Dagget shrugged. "Course not. Wasn't thinking when I was talking."

"Ain't no doubt we're getting close," the lawman continued. "Want you all to stay bunched — and see to it that you have your weapons handy. Could run into them in most any of these arroyos from here on."

"Ain't no law says they can't see us coming," Traxler mumbled. "For all we know they're just setting and waiting, guns a-pointed right at us."

The thought had occurred to Starbuck.

He rubbed at the stubble on his chin, shook his head. "Staying bunched up is wrong. We ought to spread out."

Mayo threw an angry glance at Shawn. "We stay together," he snapped. "Can put up a better fight that way, having all our guns —"

"What he says makes sense, Marshall," Traxler cut in. "They'll have us like fish in a barrel, was they to open up."

"Stay together," Mayo repeated stubbornly. "I know what I'm doing."

Abruptly a splatter of gunshots echoed through the warm afternoon air. The lawman raised his hand, quickly halted the posse.

"Where'd that come from?" Benjamin wondered, standing in his stirrups.

"Sounded like it was on ahead, close to that mountain," Davey Joe answered, also craning.

"You figure it's them?" Willard asked nervously.

"Who the hell else would be around here?" Traxler demanded impatiently. "Can't you see them tracks going right on that way?"

Shawn, studying the surrounding land, pointed to an arroyo a dozen yards to their left. It ran on a more or less direct course for the hills and was several feet below the level of the mesa across which they were moving.

"Captain, we'll get good cover down there," he said, calling it to Mayo's attention.

The lawman touched the area with an indifferent glance, resumed his contemplation of the higher ridges and canyons farther on. There was a frown of uncertainty on his weathered features, as if he were unable to decide on the next course.

They were fools to just stand there in the open, Starbuck thought, and took the matter into his own hands.

"Let's get down in the wash," he said. "Can keep out of sight while we ride closer."

He did not wait to hear any objections from the lawman, or anyone else, simply spurred the sorrel about and rode into the wide channel. The others followed immediately, and staying in the lead and keeping the gelding at a brisk walk through the loose sand, Shawn pointed for the hills.

"Smoke —"

It was Zeb Traxler's voice. Starbuck paused and glanced back at the scout. He was staring off to the south. Shawn swung his attention to that direction. A thin plume of gray was twisting up into the sky.

"Ain't no more'n a mile away."

Starbuck nodded his agreement, and roweling the sorrel, continued the slight climb of the arroyo. A time later, with the smoke ribbon now directly opposite them, he cut the big horse about and climbed out of the wash.

Gaining the flat above, he waited for the others to follow, slanting a look at the lawman as he drew in. Mayo's face was a set, angry mask. Ignoring the man, Starbuck ducked his head at the smoke.

"Coming from a sink, or a deep arroyo," he said. "Odds are it'll be the Comanchero camp. That's what we'll figure, anyway, until we know for sure."

"How we going to move in — circle around and come at them from below?" Benjamin asked, his voice tense.

"We don't — not yet. Want to see what we're up against first. Spread out in a forage line. We'll ride up quiet. When I give the signal, halt and dismount. Best we go the rest of the way on foot — maybe crawl if need be."

"Crawling — that ain't my style," Davey Joe protested. "Not for nobody."

"Then stay with the horses," Shawn replied. "Need to look down on whoever's in that arroyo without tipping our hand."

"For certain," Traxler agreed. "We go waltzing up there in plain sight and it could mean big trouble right off the bat. We best all do what the man says."

Shawn moved forward, walking the sorrel in a straight line for the wisp of smoke. Fifty yards short he halted, slipped from the saddle, and ground reining the gelding, began a cautious advance toward the grama-grass covered rim now clearly evident. The remainder of the posse, strung out to either side of him, proceeded equally quiet.

Moments later Starbuck dropped to his belly, and removing his hat, worked his way to the edge of the depression. Looking down into its considerable depth, he grunted in satisfaction. They had found the Coman-chero camp.

A surge of elation swept Davey Joe Harrison as he looked down on the outlaw camp. Here he would prove himself once and for all, show everybody — but mostly his three older brothers and his pa — that he was just as much a man — a Texan — as they figured themselves to be.

That had been his life since he became old enough to think about it — this proving something not only to those brothers in whose towering shadows he was forever being thrust, but to friends, relatives, and the outside world as well. What came easily to them, Davey Joe had to earn; and where certain things were just taken for granted by them, such as strength, ability, skill with girls and the like, he had to demonstrate.

Small like his ma, he had been the object of good-natured bullying and hoorawing by his brothers for as long as he could remember; they took after their tall, wide-shouldered pa, it was always pointed out with pride, and who — Davey Joe had heard it said so often that it now made him sick to his stomach — was a typical Texan.

Maybe so, but there was one thing they could not get around, it had been an uncle on his ma's side who'd been at the Alamo — a mighty brave man, she had told him, who was short statured like himself.

"It ain't the size that counts," she'd said when she finished telling him about it, "it's what makes up the size."

That revelation had done much to change Davey Joe's life, for he had soon embarked on a course designed to make of himself a man of note and consequence, and refute once and for all the insulting appelations tacked onto him by his brothers.

By the time he was eighteen, a juncture in life he had only recently attained, it was grudgingly conceded by all concerned that he was the fastest hand with a gun in the county, the best rider on the homestead which was slowly becoming a cattle ranch; a full-quart drinker, an expert cusser, a shark at poker, and an out-and-out whiz with the girls — all of which Davey Joe constantly reminded the world at large.

Now he was going to get his chance to do something really grand, something that would come mighty close to matching the famed exploits of that redoubtable uncle at the Alamo. In the past he'd made his brothers, and plenty of others, eat their words — now he'd give them something to chaw on the rest of their lives! When he got back home this time he might still be a foot shorter than they, but he'd be standing a hell of a lot taller!

9

Valdez had chosen well the site for his Comanchero camp. At some time in centuries past, a monstrous convulsion had shaken the earth, and when it was over, a deep bowl had been gouged from its surface. A hundred yards in width, perhaps a quarter mile in length, and with steep, unscalable walls, it lay unexpected on the fairly level land, as a ragged canyon open only narrowly at one end.

Large boulders lay scattered about on its sandy floor, and a few trees, mostly ironwood and palo-verde, along with saltbush and other scrub growth, alive despite the dearth of rainfall, were visible here and there. Several brush corrals had been erected for the livestock, and there were a dozen or more thatched lean-to affairs that evidently served as living quarters for the outlaws.

"There's them wagon-train folks —

penned up like a bunch of goats."

Mort Dagget was the first to spot the captives. Shawn followed his pointing finger, located the wagons, half hidden by one of the stock enclosures. A fence also encircled the vehicles, and looking closely, Starbuck could see several men and women, and a few children lolling about.

Ben would be among them, he realized, straining to get a better look at the prisoners, but their features were indefinite, and some were partly hidden by the wagons and the barricade itself; shortly he gave it up and turned his mind to other matters.

It would be no great problem for the captives to escape from their corral, he saw, but freedom would still be well beyond reach since they would find themselves in the center of the outlaw camp and a considerable distance from the entrance to the canyon; and with Comancheros at every hand, some dozing in the sunshine, others performing chores or just lazing about, the chances of breaking free were nil. At night there undoubtedly would be guards.

"That ain't all of Valdez' outfit," Mayo said. "No more'n a couple a dozen down there — and some of them are women. Main bunch has gone off somewheres."

"Prob'ly rode over to the mines to hash

91

things out with them jaspers that's doing the buying," Traxler said.

"Then right now'd be the time to go busting in there," Davey Joe said, his voice trembling with excitement. "Be a lead-pipe cinch."

"A head-on cavalry charge would take them by surprise," Deke Benjamin agreed.

"Be getting ourselves massacred, was you to ask me," Traxler commented in his dry, drawling way. "I figure we best come up with something better than that, don't you, Captain?"

Mayo stroked his chin. "Not much else we can do — and with them shorthanded, now'd be the time."

Adam Finch rolled over on his side, faced Starbuck. "You got any ideas?"

Shawn glanced at the sun, gauged the hour. He shook his head.

"Can't see rushing them. We'd have to come at them from the mouth of the canyon, and by the time we reached the camp they'd have seen us and be ready and waiting. Move like that could get some of the prisoners hurt, too." He paused, eyes narrowing as he studied the open end of the bowl. "They've got guards picketed there. Hadn't noticed them."

"Hell, I didn't see them birds, either,"

Traxler muttered.

"We can take care of them mighty quick," Davey Joe said. "Me and Orvy can slip up on them through all that brush and rock, slice their throats before they know what's going on."

"Maybe," Starbuck said, "but more than likely one of them would spot you in time and fire a shot — and that would tip them off for sure."

There was a long silence, and then Mayo swore impatiently. "Well, by God, I ain't just going to keep on layin' here. Come to bail out them folks and that's what I aim to."

"Goes for me, too," Starbuck said evenly. "I've got a brother down there I've been hunting for years, but it won't make much sense if I get him and myself killed just when I've finally caught up."

"How do you want to pull it off?" Kane asked, making it plain where he stood insofar as leadership of the posse was concerned.

"Wait. Be dark in two or three hours —"

"Rest of the bunch'll be back by then," Mayo cut in.

"Have to gamble on that — and if they are it'll only make the job harder. . . . Once it's dark we can slip up on the guards, like

Davey Joe said, get rid of them without making a fuss. After that it'll be a matter of moving into the camp, Apache style, and taking care of the rest of the Comancheros one or two at a time."

"Their women'll be bad as the men," Traxler said. "Like squaws. They'll kill you quick as their menfolk will."

"If we're lucky and handle it right, we ought to be able to handle them all without much of a fight. Can figure on my brother and the rest of the men from the wagon train giving us a hand."

"They won't have no guns to fight with," Dagget pointed out.

"We'll use the ones we take from the guards, and get them to the wagons fast as we can. Anybody know how many men were with the wagon train?"

"Eight or nine, near as I recollect," Finch said.

Starbuck nodded. "With that many guns we ought to be able to take care of the whole bunch —"

"Kill them — men and women both — that what you mean?" It was Davey Joe.

"Only if you have to. Take their weapons so they won't be a danger, then we can throw them in one of the corrals like they've done those people from the wagon train."

"Means we'll have to stand guard over them," Kane said.

"Could hog-tie them," Dagget suggested.

"Be the thing to do if we can manage it."

Again there was a silence. It was broken by Finch. "Well, that what we're going to do?"

"It's up to Captain Mayo, I reckon," Deke Benjamin said. "If you ask me, I think we ought to rush them right now."

"Same here," Davey Joe added. "And I'm talking for Orvy, too."

Zeb Traxler squirmed back from the edge of the canyon, sat up. "This here's something I expect every man ought to have a say in, seeing as how this ain't the army and we'll all be laying our lives on the line. How about taking a vote?"

A murmur of agreement followed the old scout's suggestion.

"All right," he said, "majority'll be the winner same as always. . . . Them of you that wants to go charging in now, say so."

"Me," Davey Joe said promptly.

"Same," Deke Benjamin added.

There was a pause and then Orvy Harrison shrugged. "Me, too."

Traxler glanced around, settled his eyes on John Mayo. The lawman was looking off into the canyon, his features hard set. The scout turned back to the others.

"Now them that wants to do it Starbuck's way."

Finch, Kane, and Dagget spoke up at once, and even Jed Willard, who had remained morosely silent and withdrawn throughout the excursion so far, voiced a quick approval. Zeb shifted his attention again to Mayo.

"I'm voting for him, too. Makes it five to three. Reckon we don't need your's, Captain, but you still got a right to have your say."

Mayo's shoulders stirred. "I'll go with the majority," he said sullenly.

Traxler studied the lawman briefly, his hawk face expressionless, and bucked his head at Starbuck.

"We'll be doing it your way. There anything that needs doing while we're waiting for dark?"

"No reason to stay here," Shawn answered. "Always a chance somebody down there might look up and spot one of us. . . . Let's cut back to the mouth of the canyon and lie low until it's time."

The men sprawled along the canyon's rim began to draw back, keeping down to avoid silhouetting against the sky.

"Like to say this now," Mayo stated as

96

they all came upright. "I'm going along with this idea because that's what most of you seem to want. If it goes haywire, like us maybe getting trapped down there by the rest of Valdez' bunch, I want it understood it ain't on my head."

"Appears to me the odds for us all coming out of this here foofaraw is about even, either way we do it," Traxler said. "Just maybe a wee mite better doing it like Starbuck wants. . . . Anyways, ain't nobody going to blame nobody for nothing, no matter how it works out."

Shawn was only half listening. He had turned, was looking off in the direction of the Comanchero camp.

"Sit tight, Ben," he murmured. "We're coming."

You couldn't expect a man who'd had no military experience to look at the situation they faced in a forthright manner. Deke Benjamin told himself as he swung onto his horse and fell in line with the rest of the posse.

Civilians never understood the mechanics of battle, thus they were poor judges of proper tactics. A hard, fast charge up that canyon, every man shooting as he rode, would make the Comanchero camp theirs

97

in mighty short order.

Certainly there would be a few losses, and no doubt some of the Luddin party would get hurt, perhaps killed, but you had to expect that. It was like General Forrest had said time and again — you don't figure the cost, you figure the gain.

He should have done some arguing about it, he supposed, pointed out that good military procedure would call for an all-out surprise attack of the sort in which he had participated many times. Some of the posse members didn't know, and likely a few of the others had forgotten that he'd been an officer in the Confederate Cavalry and had covered himself with considerable glory more than once. Forrest himself had told him one day that he ought to make the army a career, that he was a natural.

He'd given it plenty of consideration and had finally decided to do so, but then the Confederacy lost the war, and the only thing left for him to do was return home and resume selling beans and bacon to the sodbusters in that goddammed store.

Fight Indian style. Hell, that was no way for a real, genuine, red-blooded soldier! Charge the enemy, go busting straight in with guns booming, the horses' hooves setting up a regular thunder while powder smoke filled the air and bit at a man's nostrils!

That was the right way to do it — the only way, and by heaven, he just might get the rest of the posse to see it yet. He could figure on Davey Joe and Orvy — and Captain Mayo, too; it was plenty plain the old Ranger didn't like the way things had turned at all.

He'd pull Adam Finch and Dagget aside, that drunk, Willard, too, do some strong talking. He'd make them listen, and probably they'd agree with him as soon as they realized he was the only man among them with military experience.

As soon as they pulled up he'd start working on them — along with a couple of the others. They still had plenty of time to pull it off; the sun would be in their eyes, but that wouldn't be too serious a drawback.

10

Doubling back in single file, with Starbuck in the lead, the posse made its way to a brush-filled arroyo not far from the entrance to the canyon. There, in the gradually fading afternoon, the men dismounted and sought comfort on the warm sand while they awaited the moment to strike.

There was no thought of food, of having a drink of whiskey to rejuvenate flagging spirits and bolster courage; instead, a strange, tense silence, akin to that breathless hush that precedes a furious storm, possessed them.

Near sundown, Starbuck rose, removed his spurs, and motioning for the others to remain, quietly picked a course through the maze of rock, saltbush, and scrub cedars to where he could have a look at the mouth of the canyon. He spent a full hour studying the lay of the land, the positions of the guards, and all else pertinent to the area, and finally satisfied, headed back to rejoin the posse.

As he drew near, he caught the low mutter of their voices, and then, as he stepped down into the arroyo and came within view, he heard Kane say in his cold, hard-edged way: "Forget it — or you'll answer to me," after which there was only quiet.

Pulling up before them, only dimly outlined shapes in the almost complete darkness, he waited a few moments for any explanation that might be forthcoming. When none came, he assumed it was a matter of no import to him, and dropping to his haunches, began to detail his findings.

"Be no trouble to move in," he said. "Found a wash we can follow. Deep enough to keep us and the horses from being seen. Leads almost to the canyon."

"What do we do when we get there?" Finch asked.

"Want three men to go with me. Rest of you will wait with the horses while we take care of the guards. I'll hoot three times when it's done. That'll be the signal for the rest of you to come in."

"There some special place we're to meet you?"

"No, just ride straight in. We'll be waiting. Has to all be done quiet — remember that.

101

Can't afford to tip off the rest of the camp."

"What three are you picking to go with you?" Zeb Traxler asked.

"Asking for volunteers. That's the way this started, we'll keep it on the same basis."

"I'm going —" Davey Joe said promptly. "Orvy, too."

Shawn frowned. He would prefer to have the older men with him. Davey Joe, in his rashness, could cause trouble, but he had committed himself and there was no changing it now. The problem resolved itself, however, within the next few moments, every member of the party made his request to be included.

"Proper thing to do," Adam Finch said, "is draw straws. Three short ones go."

"That's the ticket," Traxler said, and reached for a dry branch lying nearby. Breaking it into the required number and lengths, he dropped them into his hat. Rising, he made a circuit of the men, allowed each to draw quickly from the battered headpiece.

Davey Joe . . . Willard . . . Deke Benjamin.

Starbuck nodded as each of the three held up his shortened twig. His personal selection would have been different, would have included Jim Kane and Adam Finch, and probably Zeb Traxler, but he guessed it didn't really matter; as always he would be relying mostly upon himself, anyway.

"Plan's simple," he said. "You all remember what the camp looked like. It's a box canyon with the Comancheros and the Luddin party at the far end — the west side.

"We'll be coming in from the east. The entrance is fifty feet or so wide. Slopes on both sides are steep and covered with rocks and brush. When we get there we'll split up, two of us to each side. Rest of you'll be holding the horses and waiting for my signal."

"There still two sentries posted on each side?" Benjamin asked.

"Near as I could tell."

John Mayo hawked, spat. "Seems to me it'd be a better idea for us all to take them guards. Be five of us to their two."

"Thought of that, but ten men climbing around through the rocks and bushes are bound to set up a racket," Starbuck replied.

"Any sign of Valdez and the others?" Mort Dagget wanted to know.

Starbuck shook his head. "Didn't see any change in the camp, but it was getting dark and I couldn't make out things too good. We would've heard them ride in."

"What do you want us to do if they show up?" the squat, one-time stagecoach driver continued. "Come in after you?"

"Don't do anything," Shawn said, quietly. "We'll know it as soon as you do and look out for ourselves. Best you stay put so's we'll know where you are." He paused, looked around. "Any more questions?"

"Just one," Davey Joe said in a reckless sort of way. "When are we opening this ball?"

"Now," Shawn replied, drawing upright. "Lead your horses."

Moving off to where the sorrel waited, he took the horse's reins in his right hand and headed off along the course he'd earlier chosen. Behind him he heard the muted movements of the posse as they swung in behind him, each man again utterly silent, with only the squeak of leather and the faint crunch of sand beneath the hooves of his mount marking his passage.

Starbuck continued on at a fair pace until he reached a point where the mouth of the canyon was visible. There he swung up out of the wash and halted in a fairly dense stand of cedars.

"Here's where you wait," he said, addressing his words to the party in general as he passed the sorrel's leathers to Traxler, immediately to his left. He glanced at the riders selected by chance to accompany him.

All had relinquished their horses and were moving up to him.

"Be needing a knife," he said. "Guns are out. A shot would finish it off for us."

Davey Joe patted the long blade hanging from his belt. Benjamin nodded, touched his sheathed weapon. Jed Willard stirred, looked about. Orvy Clark drew the knife he was carrying, passed it to the older man.

"Can use mine if you like —"

Willard, features stiff, took the weapon in his hand, held it gingerly at his side. Shawn studied him closely. Jed was the one who'd lost his family in an Indian massacre, someone had said. The incident had hit him hard.

"Looks like you maybe don't feel up to doing a lot of climbing around in the dark," he said, kindly. "Expect one of the others would be willing to take your place."

Willard stirred angrily. "Nope, I'm fine. . . . Just this here waiting around."

"Know what you mean," Starbuck said. "Always the worst part." He shifted his attention to Benjamin and Davey Joe. "Jed and I'll circle and cross to the other side. Give us about ten minutes to get set."

"Better give us some kind of a signal so we'll know," the redhead suggested.

"All right. I'll use an owl hoot again —

two times. When you hear that, start closing in."

"And when we've got our part done, we'll hoot back," Benjamin said.

"Agreed," Starbuck said, and started to turn away. Abruptly he halted. "There's no guarantee that there's only two guards on each side. Could be I didn't spot them all, so watch yourself, and take nothing for granted."

"Don't you worry none," Davey Joe said confidently. "Two or four — or six, it's all the same to me and Deke."

Shawn glanced at the older man. The redhead's shoulders twitched. "I'll look out for him," he murmured.

Starbuck moved off into the night with Jed Willard at his side, taking a course through the brush that led directly away from the canyon. It was not hard going. They shortly dropped into a shallow wash where the soft, loose sand offered comfortable footing.

A fair distance from the canyon's entrance he cut due south, and with Jed Willard still totally silent at his shoulder, doubled back, halting finally at the foot of the lower slope marking the mouth of the opening. Touching Willard on the arm, Starbuck pointed to a dark mass of shrubbery a bit to the east of the opposite incline.

"Things go wrong and we get separated," he said in a low voice, "that's where the rest of the posse is waiting. Head for there."

Jed Willard signaled his understanding.

Shawn turned his attention to the grade lifting before them. "Guards'll be on the other side of this hill," he said, reaching into his left boot and drawing a long, slim-bladed knife. "They'll likely be asleep, but we won't bank on it. Aim to climb to the top, get them spotted, and then move in. Understand?"

Willard said, "Sure," in a hoarse whisper. "When are you giving the signal?"

"You ready?"

"Reckon I am — ready as I'll ever be."

Starbuck turned toward the distant brush beyond the canyon's entrance. Cupping a hand about his lips, he hooted softly.

"Let's go," he said then, and stepping by Willard, began to carefully pick his way up the grade.

Here goes nothing, Jed Willard thought as he stepped in behind Starbuck and began to climb the grade. He was damn glad it was the big, square-jawed gunslinger, if that's what he was, had drawn him as a partner. He sure hadn't wanted that crazy kid, Davey Joe — and as for Deke Benjamin, well, he was loco too, but in a different way.

Not that it made a hell of a lot of difference as to how it all turned out. Life had ended for him that morning when he'd walked into what remained of his house and saw what the Kiowas had done to Nellie and the boys. Nothing ever really mattered after that, never would in fact, other than how to get his hands on another bottle of booze, which was the only way he could blot out the memories that kept sifting back into his head.

That fellow Kane, he wouldn't have been a bad one to line up with, though; he was a lot like Starbuck, and you knew the moment you took a look at him that he was all business and meant what he said. He'd cooled down Benjamin mighty fast when Deke started talking to them all about taking over the bossing of the posse from Starbuck and charging the Comanchero camp hell-for-leather like they would've done in the war.

But again, he wouldn't have cared much about the outcome of a fool stunt like that, it was only that he wouldn't like to see a man like Starbuck get double-crossed. He was glad Kane had felt the same way and made a stand. He wouldn't have had the guts himself.

Jed glanced ahead. Starbuck was a couple of yards ahead of him. The climb was a steep one and he was beginning to feel the strain in his legs and had to suck a bit hard for breath. He reckoned he could thank all that rot-gut whiskey he'd drunk in the past for that — whiskey and poor eating and never a good night's sleep.

Maybe, after all this was over, he could try to change a bit. Perhaps doing something good would help him get back on his feet and give him a start at living like a man ought to. Being around somebody like Starbuck, who didn't look at you like you were something that needed stepping on and squashing in spite of what he'd been told about you, sort of woke up the hope in you and set you to thinking. Could be, if he'd put his mind to it, he could start over, find some kind of a better life for himself.

Willard paused. Starbuck had halted, was looking back at him, evidently having heard him wheezing like a wind-broke bronc. Raising a hand, he waved the big trail-rider on. He wasn't going to be the one who held back the party — not if he busted a blood vessel keeping up.

"Keep going," he said.

11

The slope was steep, cluttered with rock and brush. Starbuck, carefully choosing a path, suddenly became aware of Willard's harsh breathing. He stopped, looked around.

At once the older man said, "Keep going," in a low voice.

Shawn resumed the ascent, and at a slower pace began to veer to his right. The guards should be just over the brow of the hill, unless they had changed positions. If that proved to be true, it meant searching them out, which would not only be risky but time consuming.

Far off in the black-velvet night a coyote yelped, the sound carrying endlessly through the low hills and across the lonely flats. Willard muttered something and again Shawn halted, wanting to give him a few moments of needed rest; but the man would not accept the break, seemingly determined to uphold his end with no favors asked or taken.

Abruptly the crest lay before them, a thin, rounded ridge upon which stunted shrubbery and fair-sized rocks rose stark against the moonless sky. Starbuck paused, laid a cautioning hand on Willard's shoulder.

Smoke . . . tobacco smoke. . . . Shawn, hunched behind one of the boulders, searched the slope below him for a sign of the Comanchero. A small, red eye glowed vividly, faded, came alive again. . . . The tip of the guard's cigarette alternately going bright and dull in the darkness as it was puffed. . . . Back in the depths of the sink where the camp lay, a man shouted, and then a laugh drifted hollowly through the void.

Starbuck, knife in hand, touched Jed Willard again, pointed to his left. With a finger, drawing a half circle in the cool air, he indicated to the man that he was to work down-slope, come in on the guard from the side. He would follow a similar procedure on the outlaw's opposite flank.

Willard bobbed his head, moved off silently. Shawn, cutting back along the crest for a few paces, began to thread his way downgrade toward the outlaw, hidden from him, at that moment, by a shoulder of rock jutting from the slope.

Across the way, Deke Benjamin and Davey Joe would be, or at least should be, closing in on the Comancheros posted on that side of the canyon's entrance. The younger man still worried him to some extent; he was so anxious to make a hero of himself, he could upset the entire plan. Benjamin could control the boy if he would trouble himself to do so.

The smell of the cigarette reached him again. Shawn halted, drew up flat against the bulge of granite. Straining, he probed the dimness ahead. Then he saw the outlaw, a dark shape slumped against a rock; each time he sucked on his cigarette, his swarthy, shining face became apparent.

Where was the second guard?

Anxious, Shawn eyed the area around the man. Visibility was less than poor. Even the stars were shut out by an overcast. A rock rattled on the slope . . . Willard.

At once the Comanchero drew himself erect, turned to the sound. Starbuck silently rounded the shoulder of rock, moved in swiftly. His arm rose, then fell. The outlaw gasped, collapsed into a heap.

Listening, Shawn crouched beside the man, poised for any noise that would indicate the presence of the other Comanchero.

None came. Pulling the bandoleer of cartridges from the outlaw's limp shoulders, Starbuck slung it over his own, and taking up the rifle dropped to the sand and crept forward to a lower mound of rock.

He'd lost track of Jed Willard completely — and still had no idea where the second Comanchero was posted. Grim, senses keyed to their peak, he hunched beside the boulders. Across on the opposite slope an owl hooted twice. He felt the tension pushing through him slacken. Davey Joe and Deke Benjamin had completed their part of the plan, and were now awaiting his signal that he and Willard had accomplished theirs.

Where the hell was Willard — and where was the other guard? Could there be only one on the slope? Almost immediately he heard the sound of sliding gravel and then the muffled report of a pistol. Immediately he hurried forward, pointing for the source of the activity which was apparently just beyond a dense clump of brush. He reached there, halted. Two shadowy figures lay motionless on the ground.

Crossing quickly to them, Shawn knelt. Jed Willard, big knife clutched in both hands, was sprawled across the outlaw. The odor of burning cloth was in the air and he could see that the front of Willard's linsey-woolsey shirt was afire.

Starbuck hastily rolled the man to his back, pinched out the flames, and felt for a pulse. There was none. He turned then to the Comanchero. Orvy Clark's thick-bladed weapon was hilt deep in the outlaw's chest.

It was not difficult to reconstruct what had taken place. Jed, moving up through the darkness, had stumbled onto the second guard. Both, equally startled, had reacted instantly. Willard, in a successful effort to deaden the sound of the pistol blast, had thrown himself against its muzzle while driving his blade into the outlaw's body. Both undoubtedly had died instantly.

Starbuck, collecting the weapons, got to his feet, and for a time looked down at Willard's stilled features. He'd been a man afraid, yet he hadn't hesitated to spend his life when it was necessary. Wheeling then, he turned back toward the mouth of the canyon. They could pick up Jed Willard's body later, when it was all over, and give him a decent burial, or if so decided, pack the body back to Sabine Springs. He'd leave it up to the others. Pausing briefly, he gave the signal for the posse to move in and continued on down the slope.

Benjamin and Davey Joe were waiting when he reached the sandy floor of the canyon. The redhead came forward to meet him.

"Where's Willard?" he asked immediately.

"Dead," Starbuck replied, and gave his version of what had happened.

Deke shook his head. Davey Joe, abruptly sober in the face of their first casualty, murmured, "Poor old Jed."

Shawn glanced toward the narrow gatelike opening at the end of the canyon. He could hear the horses coming into it. "That gunshot reach you?"

Benjamin shook his head. "No."

"Wouldn't have been heard in the camp then," Starbuck said, and turned to the approaching riders.

When they had drawn abreast, he took the reins of the sorrel from Jim Kane and went to the saddle. Silent until Deke Benjamin and Davey Joe had repeated his account of Willard's death, he then swung about to face the men.

"Makes us short one hand," he said in a heavy voice as he returned the knife Willard had borrowed to its owner. "Can't afford to lose another. It clear what we're doing next?"

"Working our way into the camp, that's what," Zeb Traxler said tautly. "And I'm aiming to collect me two, maybe three scalps for Jed."

"Same here," Davey Joe announced. "Maybe Jed Willard was a no-account, but he was a Texan and worth a half-a-dozen of them thieving Comancheros that —"

"Don't lose your head," Starbuck cut in. "Take it as it comes, slow and careful. Like as not everybody'll be asleep — which will make it some easier. Just move in, do what you have to do."

"We taking prisoners?" Kane asked.

"Leaving that up to you — but I don't see a need for wholesale murder. Main thing is we want every outlaw in there disarmed and in no shape to give us trouble. . . . Be plenty of rope around, I expect. Tie them up and throw them in one of the corrals like they've done those folks from the wagon train. Everybody set?"

There was a murmur of assent. Shawn put the sorrel into a slow walk along the edge of the canyon's floor, avoiding the open center. They had succeeded so far in keeping their presence a secret and he was taking no chance now on someone in the camp glancing in their direction, and seeing riders approaching, sounding an alarm.

He came to the first of the brush-fenced yards. A dozen or so horses loomed up dimly within it. At once Shawn halted and

116

dismounted. The others quietly followed his example, with weapons ready they gathered around him. Reaching out, he touched Benjamin, Traxler, Mayo, Davey Joe, and Dagget on the shoulders.

"Take the other side," he murmured. "Good luck."

The men replied softly, moved off into the murky night. Starbuck waited until he was certain they had gained the opposite wall of the canyon, and then nodding to the remaining members of the posse, said, "Let's go."

It was absurdly easy. At the first jacal, Kane stepped inside and used the butt of his pistol on the two men sprawled on a straw mat beneath the thatched roof. Removing their weapons, he rejoined the others, all following a like procedure. Across the way, now somewhat lighted by a smouldering fire, the remaining members of the party were progressing steadily also.

Two women created a problem in one of the lean-tos near the fenced-in area where the wagon-train people were being held, but Finch and Orvy together quickly subdued the pair, and then with strips obtained by ripping up a blanket, bound and gagged them securely.

Elsewhere in the camp were occasional sounds of scuffling, all quickly over, however, and shortly after, Starbuck, tense anticipation mounting within him as he realized the long search for his brother was only moments from coming to an end, halted. In front of him was the stockadelike corral in which the prisoners were being held. The rounded, canvas tops of the wagons showed whitely in the night and the lone guard slumped against the crude, woven brush gate was asleep. Before Shawn could act, Kane stepped by him and quietly and efficiently removed the outlaw and drew back the barrier.

Starbuck stepped hurriedly into the enclosed area. Several men lay asleep beneath and alongside the vehicles. The women and children, he reckoned, were inside. Crossing to the nearest pallet, he shook the man awake, unconsciously holding his hand over the fellow's mouth.

"It's all right," he said quietly, "we're friends. Posse from Sabine Springs. We've come after you."

The man, an elderly individual with gray hair, sighed deeply. "Thank God," he murmured. "We've been praying somebody would. . . . I'm Tom Luddin. How many in your party?"

"Nine. . . . We've got weapons for all of you."

Shawn paused, glanced around at the other men, disturbed by their conversation and rousing slowly. In the darkness their features were indistinguishable.

"Your scout — man by the name of Friend — where is he?" Starbuck's voice was tight, sounded unnatural in his own ears.

"Gone," Luddin replied.

Traxler watched Starbuck and the three posse members, the lucky ones, fade off into the dark. He would have given up his claim on a cool corner in hell to be one of them, but sometimes the cards just didn't fall the way a man would like.

"That jackleg'll get them all killed," he heard John Mayo say.

The lawman was looking plenty beat, Zeb had noticed earlier, and there seemed to be a lot of pain showing in his eyes, but there'd been no complaining.

"I doubt that, Captain," he said. "I figure they'll do fine."

"Same here," Mort Dagget put in. "Ain't no corncobs in that Starbuck fellow's head. . . . Got a plenty of guts, too —"

"Guts!" Mayo echoed. "What the hell you know about guts? From what I —"

"Ease up you two," Traxler said mildly, cutting a chunk off his plug of Mule and poking it into his mouth. "You're sounding like a couple of quarreling kids."

The lawman shook his head wearily, pulled off his hat. "Expect I am a bit jumpy. Just that I ain't liking the way things're going. I'm supposed to be running this posse —"

"Reckon that's what's chewing on you, ain't it, Captain," Traxler asked, maneuvering the bit of tobacco about with his tongue to a more manageable position between cheek and teeth. "And it's a burning your britches."

"I'm responsible for —"

"Sure you are, but you're a dang fool to let that fog up your thinking. . . . You best face up to something, John, we ain't young as we once was, and there's young fellows growed up all around us that's just as smart as we ever was — maybe smarter. You got to expect it.

"Now, I figure a man's going to live 'til he dies, and that'll come along in due time. Meanwhile, he best ride along, when he's old as you and me, and if there's some young squirt comes sashaying up all full of stuff and vinegar and honing to take over, I say let him.

"I've done paid my dues in this life, so I ain't about to begrudge somebody like this here Starbuck grabbing the leathers and taking hold — and you ought to be feeling the same.

"I got a hunch you're fooling yourself, John, and that's the worst thing a man can do to hisself. I think you best remember — the days that are behind us are something you can't change. Last year is a year gone and there sure ain't no way you can back up and do it over."

12

"Gone!" Starbuck echoed in a stricken voice, as frustration and a sort of anger rolled through him. "Where?"

"For help," Luddin replied. "Was about noon today. He heard some of them Mexicans talking — seems he can understand their lingo — and found out there was a troop of soldiers somewheres to the south of here. Went looking for them."

"How'd he manage to escape?"

"Knocked one of the guards on the head when he came in here. Put on his clothes and got on a horse and just rode out."

A faint smile pulled at Shawn's lips. "He got away with that?"

"Far as I know. Just about the time he was going out the end of the sink somebody hollered at him. Then there was some shooting."

Those had been the gunshots he and the posse had heard, Starbuck realized. "He

122

get hit?"

"Don't think so because about a half-a-dozen of them Mexicans mounted up and took off after him. Ain't come back yet."

Starbuck remained motionless, eyes reaching off into the blackness beyond the camp, now brightening as wood thrown onto the fire by some of the party began to flame. Around him there was steady activity. The posse, under the direction of John Mayo, reasserting his command, was completing the take-over of the camp, herding and dragging, when necessary, the now captive Comancheros, and placing them inside a stout corral built against the canyon's steep wall.

The women of the wagon train were now up and standing about, blankets pulled about them to ward off the night's chill while they conversed quietly. A child was crying inside one of the vehicles.

"We got them all — 'cepting the dead ones — rounded up and put in a pen," Davey Joe reported, halting beside Starbuck. "You want us to get ready to head back for the border?"

Shawn brought his thoughts of Ben to a stop. The majority of the posse had followed young Harrison into the corral, and like him, were awaiting his orders. He turned to

Luddin.

"You got any idea when Valdez and the rest of his bunch will be back?"

"Sometime this morning. Leastwise that's what Friend said. . . . You asked about him — he something to you?"

"A brother. How many in the party?"

"Was about two dozen of them rode out. Left a little over half that many here to look after us."

"We got eight men and six women prisoners," Finch said. "Was no kids."

"Never is," Traxler explained. "Kids and old women and them that's in a family way have to stay in the main camp. It's a sort of permanent home. This here's only a roosting place they use while they're working this part of the country."

"Had to be more'n half the bunch left here," Benjamin said. "Was six rode off after Starbuck's brother. We killed four of them getting into the canyon, maybe a half a dozen more taking over. Then there's eight that's inside that stockade —"

"Was only guessing," Luddin said with a shrug. "Kind of hard to keep track, them all kind of looking alike and us cooped up the way we've been. . . . Hadn't we best start loading the wagons?"

Starbuck gave that thought. Valdez and

the remainder of his Comanchero gang were due back in only a few hours. Even if he and the posse headed out with the wagon train immediately, they'd not get far before the outlaws caught up with them — and their chances for fighting off a large force of outlaws would be slim. Too, Ben had apparently made a successful escape and had gone to fetch the Federalistas; they could be on the way at that very moment.

Shawn swung his attention to Luddin. "How many in your party?"

"Well, there's me and my sons," he said, jerking a thumb at two husky blond men in their early twenties standing off to the side. "And there's their wives and youngsters. Got three little ones apiece. Then we got Tait Lawton and his missus, and Abe Wagner and his'n. They got a daughter, Carla. She's going on seventeen, as I recollect."

Shawn totaled the count: five men, four women, six small children and a young girl. There would be no traveling fast with them even if they left the wagons behind and rode horseback.

"You say Damon Friend's your brother?" the man called Lawton asked. "Name ain't the same —"

"Brothers just the same," Starbuck replied and glanced at Davey Joe and Orvy. They

125

had discovered Carla Wagner, a small, elfin like brunette who was carrying on an animated conversation with them near a second fire now burning brightly in the corral.

"What about it?" Mort Dagget pressed worriedly. "We getting out of here? We're sort of pushing our luck, standing around like this. Ought to get going."

"Maybe," Shawn said, "but I'm wondering how far we'll get before Valdez and his bunch catches up with us."

Finch glanced up quickly. "Never thought of that! Sure ain't going to be making no time with folks like these."

"Was what we came for, wasn't it?" Benjamin said. "Why're we holding back now?"

One of the women came up, offered Starbuck a cup of coffee. "Hard to tell you how much we're thanking you," she murmured. "More'n any of us can put in words."

He smiled, nodded, and watched idly as two more of the wives moved by, one carrying a number of battered cups, the other a pot from which the good smell of hot coffee was filtering. They passed the containers to other members of the posse and filled them to the brim with the steaming liquid.

"We ain't," Mayo declared suddenly in a firm voice, bucking his head at Deke Benjamin. "Longer we stall around here the closer Valdez'll get." Pivoting on a heel, he faced Luddin and his followers. "Want you people ready to pull out in an hour — less if possible. Need to be as far from here as we can get, come sunup —"

"Which won't be far enough," Starbuck said quietly. "Best thing we can do is stay right here."

13

A stunned silence followed his words, one broken only by the crackling of wood in the fires. Finally Tom Luddin found his voice.

"You saying we're just going to wait here, let them outlaws —"

"No, sir!" the lawman snapped, pushing up close to Starbuck. "We ain't doing no such a damned thing. Be same as setting here in a trap!"

"About all it was from the beginning," Shawn said coolly. "Figured you all knew that."

"What's that mean?"

"Coming here with ten men and expecting to just ride right in and out with these people — what did you figure the Comancheros would be doing all that time?"

"Was expecting a fight," Deke Benjamin said, "and we're ready and willing. Anyways, you come along, didn't you?"

"I did, and I'd have come alone if you all

hadn't been making the ride —"

"Then what the hell's all the yammering about?" Adam Finch demanded impatiently.

"About what a tomfool stunt it'd be leaving here with a bunch of women and kids and trying to get to the border before Valdez and his bunch can catch us," Zeb Traxler said. "Starbuck's right again. We'd never make it."

"If we left now we could cover plenty of ground before the Comancheros showed up," Mayo said, his manner less positive.

"No guarantee of that," Starbuck said. "We don't know when they'll ride in — could be before daylight, or maybe it'll be noon. Way I see it, if they show up anytime sooner than dark, we'd be in trouble."

"There's nine of us and there's five of these wagon-train folks that can shoot," Davey Joe pointed out. "I reckon we could put up a pretty good scrap."

"Against a couple-a-dozen outlaws?"

"Probably be more'n that," Traxler said, shifting his cud. "My guess is we'd need about a two-day start to beat them to the border, slowed down bad like we'll be."

"And there sure ain't no place between here and there where we could make a stand," Finch said, beginning to understand the situation. "Can see now what Starbuck's driving at."

"Can't say as I do," Mayo snapped. "We rode in here after these people, now he's telling us we'll be fools if we try to get them out."

Shawn glanced at the Luddin party. They were standing a bit apart, listening intently and taking no part in the discussion. One of the younger men had thrown more wood on the fires. In their ruddy reflection their features were strained, worried.

"I'm saying it would be a mistake to head out across country with them," he said. "That would end up with all of us being prisoners — or dead."

"So what's the answer?"

"We sit tight. If my brother had any luck at all, he'll be showing up with that troop of Mexican cavalry —"

"Hell!" somebody exploded. "I plumb forgot about him!"

"No guarantee either that he found them, but it looks like he got away, and that makes the odds better than good."

"What'll we be doing in the meantime?" Mayo's tone was again harsh, scornful. "Valdez and them'll be riding in. If he gets here before your brother and the Federalistas, we'll be worse off than ever."

"Not figuring on letting him ride in,"

Starbuck answered.

There was another lengthy pause. Over in the stockade, where the few Comancheros had been imprisoned, some sort of disturbance had broken out, a wild thrashing about punctuated by yelling and talking in shrill Spanish. Dagget wheeled, trotted over to the enclosure, had a quick look. He returned at once, shook his head to indicate that nothing of consequence was taking place.

"Now, how you aim to do that?" the lawman asked, his tone still skeptical. "One minute you're telling us we can't fight off Valdez, next minute you're the same as saying we can."

"That's right. We'd not have a chance in the open, but here in this box canyon we can hold him off, maybe for days — at least until the army shows up."

"If it shows up —"

"I'll admit we'll be gambling on that, but the way I see it we don't have much choice. We can't outrun Valdez for sure, but we can fort up, make our stand right here and hope the Federalistas are on the way."

Once more there was a hush. Tom Luddin rubbed at his jaw, wagged his head. "What if they ain't? What if your brother didn't find them soldiers, or maybe got hisself

131

killed by that bunch that went chasing after him; then what?"

"Swim that river when we come to it —"

"Well, I got all these folks to be worrying about," Luddin said with a long sigh. "I can't settle for maybes and things like that. Need something more to go on."

"Could be you'd as soon we'd move on, let you work it out by yourself," Traxler said, his tone dry and acid. "We come here risking ourselves to help and you —"

Shawn raised a hand, silenced the old scout. "Not what he's getting at, Zeb."

"Sure'n hell what it sounded like to me! You pegged it right when you said we put our necks on the chopping block when we took on the chore of going after these folks. I figure they could be a mite more thankful to us."

"We are — and a plenty," Luddin said. "I'm right sorry you took what I said wrong. Lord knows you men are the answers to our prayers, and whether we come out of this alive or not we're more'n grateful to you. It's just that folks like us are different from you all. We have to have something to go on."

"Like what? A man don't get no for-sures on anything in this life."

"Just what I'm trying to say. We don't look

at things the same as you folks in this part of the country do. You people just sort of take things as they come — good or bad. We're the kind that see it another way. We have to have hope and be able to look ahead and know there's something better waiting for us somewhere.

"Take our womenfolk, they couldn't stand all the hardships we've gone through and'll be going through if they wasn't able to think we'd find a better life some day soon. Reckon that sort of goes for us men, too. We got to keep up the faith in ourselves and in God, and keep thinking things'll turn out all right in the end. Expect, was we to decide there was nothing ahead for us, we'd plain quit."

"Amen," one of the women murmured.

"Well, I think we ought to be putting our faith and trust in Mr. Starbuck," the girl, Carla, said moving up to stand beside Tom Luddin. "I think he can get us out of here."

The leader of the wagon train frowned, looked down at the girl. One of the other older men, evidently her father, shook his head.

"This is not women's business —"

"Why isn't it? We're a part of this same as you and the men." Carla paused and glanced back over her shoulder to the women, as if seeking confirmation. None of them spoke up.

"You don't have to worry none, Missy!" Davey Joe said, his voice strong and confident. "We're getting you all out of here, one way or another. Can figure on it. If that Mex army doesn't show up, we'll think of something else."

Starbuck smiled. Zeb Traxler snorted, spat. "You best start working on that right now, youngster. Rest of us don't plan on it being all that easy."

"Ain't saying it will be, just saying that there'll be a way. Always is."

"Sure. We can all grab us up a shovel apiece and dig us a tunnel clear to the border," the old scout said sarcastically.

"Aw, there ain't no sense in that kind of talk —"

Someone in the crowd laughed, broke the tension. Mayo pulled off his hat, swore wearily. "Well, we need to be doing something."

Kane nodded, turned to Starbuck. "What do you want done?"

"Need to fortify the place, fix it up so's fourteen of us can hold off Valdez and however many men he's got with him. . . . Not too much we can do right now about that on account of the dark, but it'll be first light soon and we can begin. Meantime, it would be smart to dig up all the weapons and ammunition we can, put them where they'll be handy."

Davey Joe, a wide smile on his face, nodded happily. "This here's going to be just like the Alamo," he said.

A man can slip one time and forever wear a brand, Mort Dagget thought morosely as he hunched, shoulders to a rock, just beyond the flare of the firelight. Nearby the women of the Luddin party were going about the task of cooking up breakfast for all to eat, while other members of the posse and the wagon-train men stood about and talked over what should be done to prepare the camp for a siege as soon as it was light enough to work.

He was taking no part in the discussion, partly because time and events had developed within him a sense of being unwelcome among others, but mostly on account of the way town Marshal John Mayo looked at him. The lawman knew about him, he was certain, but he didn't know all that had happened that day when the stagecoach was held up in Baxter Pass and four men were killed. Nobody alive did.

He usually rode shotgun for the coach,

but that day he was handling the lines, the regular driver, Enos Church, being down with the grippe. On the box beside him was a substitute guard, Harley Trevison, a fellow he'd met only once before. They were carrying three passengers, all men, and a box carrying a twelve thousand dollar payroll consigned to the Arizona Queen Mine.

Six masked riders had hit them just as they topped out the pass and the first man shot was Trevison. Two of the horses went down at the same moment, the coach jackknifed and flopped over on its side and the next thing he knew he was standing in the middle of the road with four dead bodies strewn about him in the dust, the payroll box gone, and a dozen men wearing deputy sheriff badges staring at him coldly from their saddles.

Later they said there was little doubt as to what had taken place. When the road agents struck, he'd jumped from his seat and hid out in the brush, making no effort to protect his passengers and the shipment of cash. Proof? There wasn't any — only it was damn funny everybody else ended up dead and he didn't have a scratch save for a small lump on his head which he probably gave himself. There'd even been a few dark hints that he'd been in on the robbery himself, had made it easy for the outlaws.

There was proof of nothing, however, and so no charges were ever filed, but the company had let him go, cutting him loose in a world where his name was anathema; everywhere he went seeking work at the only trade at which he was proficient he was rebuffed, and with each refusal the cynicism and deep bitterness within him grew stronger.

He was a loser, jinxed — a nothing with no prospect of a future. He sent his wife back home to live with her folks, promising to send for her as soon as he found a job — now any kind of a job — but the blot on his record, despite a change of name for a time, persisted in all walks of endeavor and he found himself fortunate to get even the most menial work, and that for only as long as it took for someone to recognize him, and remember.

He'd been hanging around Sabine Springs when the Luddin wagon train passed through on its way to the Pecos country. When word came of its kidnapping by the Comancheros, and Mayo had called for volunteers to make up a posse, he'd stepped forward. The old lawman had been giving him a fishy eye ever since he'd hit town. Mort figured he knew from the letters the stage company had put out, or from newspaper accounts, who he was, or at least had a strong hunch. But Mayo had never said anything, and now in need of men, had allowed him to mount up with the rest willing to ride.

This was the last go-around as far as he was concerned. He was tired of the fight, of bucking odds that were insurmountable, and if things didn't go right this time, he was ready to quit. All he wanted was a chance to convince others that he wasn't yellow and had not turned tail and run that day in Baxter Pass, and more importantly, to prove it to himself.

As far as he could remember, he'd been knocked cold and thrown into the brush when the coach went over — but he didn't know for sure. His recollection of those moments was hazy and incomplete. He didn't think he was a coward, and if it turned out he wasn't — who better to prove it before than onetime Ranger, Captain John Mayo? If he was, well, it wouldn't matter.

14

By the time the sun had broken over the eastern horizon and begun its climb through a still, cloud-troubled sky, Starbuck and the men had set to work.

All of the weapons and ammunition taken from the captive outlaws had been collected and placed at a central point, and every man was now armed. The wagons, which some thought should be placed in the entrance to the canyon as a means for blocking it, were left where they stood.

"We move them," Shawn explained, "it'll be a sure tip-off to Valdez that something's wrong."

He had turned then to Dagget, waiting nearby. "Need a lookout on the rim —"

"That's me," Mort replied promptly.

Starbuck nodded. "Take your horse and find a high place up there where you've got a long view of the country. Quick as you spot Valdez come riding in, give me the word. Don't try yelling or firing your gun as a signal. The Comancheros'll hear it for sure."

"On my way," Dagget said. He trotted off to where their mounts were corralled.

Elsewhere along the floor of the canyon, members of the posse, aided by Luddin and his sons and friends, were completing the chore of erecting barricades, making use of the larger rocks and plentiful brush. The one requirement Starbuck had established was that the shelters be big enough for two men and that they afford protection from all sides since they could expect to be fired down upon from the encircling rim of the canyon.

"Somebody's going to have to keep an eye on them prisoners," Zeb Traxler said as he and Shawn made a careful tour of the walls, making certain there were no trails cutting down them from the mesa above.

"We will at that," Shawn agreed. "One of them needs only to holler loud enough for Valdez to hear and we've lost our edge — and the way things stand, we need all the help we can manage."

The old scout spat. "Still better'n getting caught out there on the flats where they could cut us to pieces. Why don't you put them two boys in there to watching them?

140

With them both toting big knives, and Davey Joe all the time acting like he's just honing to cut your throat, they ought to be able to keep that bunch quiet."

"Good choice, but when Valdez shows up and things get started we'll need their guns," Starbuck said and then hesitated. "Be a mistake to turn our backs on them altogether. If they got out they'd cause plenty of trouble. Expect we'd best leave somebody at the gate."

"That's a job for Orvy. Davey Joe's more of a fighter."

Shawn said, "Fine. Be obliged to you if you'll set it up with them."

"Sure thing," Traxler replied, and hurried off.

Starbuck completed his inspection tour and halted, satisfied. They could have no fear of any Comanchero slipping into the camp from the rim. There was no possible way, of course, to prevent the outlaws from taking up positions along its ragged course and shooting down upon the entrenched men, but he had provided for that probability already in the arrangement of the barricades scattered along the floor of the sink.

Water. . . . He'd best see to their supply. Turning on a heel, he doubled back to where the two wagons were standing. The women were busily preparing food, getting stocked ahead so there would be no necessity to cook and thus endanger themselves once the shooting began. All had been instructed to immediately find shelter under the wagons when the outlaws put in their appearance. Stepping up to a barrel setting beside the nearest wagon, he rapped sharply on its side. It was half full.

"This all the water you've got?" he asked, glancing around.

The women paused. Carla Wagner wiped her hands on her apron, smiled at him. "There's another barrel over there," she said, and pointed to the second vehicle.

He followed her to the opposite side of the canvas-topped Studebaker, sounded out the contents of the cask roped securely to a platform extending from its side. It was almost full.

"They made us fill them when we forded the river," Carla said.

If she was worried about what lay ahead for her and her people, she did not show it. She was bright and cheerful, was taking everything as if it were a day no different from any other in her life. He wondered if she actually realized what would happen if they failed to hold out against the Comancheros. He shrugged. Undoubtedly she did; Carla was a smart girl.

He shifted his attention to the brush shelters the outlaws had built, swept them with his glance. "Where have they been getting their water? With all the stock they've got penned up they need plenty. Have to have some for themselves, too."

Carla was staring up at him, arms folded, head cocked slightly, interest filling her eyes.

"There's a creek or maybe a spring around here somewheres close," she answered after a bit. "They drove the horses out three days ago, then brought them back. Were gone most of the morning. Pa figured they'd been taken to water. The men had those goatskin water bags of theirs full, too."

Starbuck gave that thought. If there was a source for water in the area they'd have no way of getting to it once the outlaws returned; and he doubted there was time enough left now to search it out.

"Going to have to make do with what we've got," he said. "Like for you to pass the word on to the other women."

Carla nodded. "I'll tell them. Have you got everything else ready?"

"Much as we can —"

"I'm thankful you're the one in charge!" She blurted the words, cutting into his

143

reply. "At noon — will you come and eat with me — my folks?"

Starbuck studied the girl closely. "There some special reason?"

"Well, no — I'd just like to talk. I heard some of the others telling about you, how you'd been everywhere, seen so much. . . ."

"Appreciate the offer," Shawn said, smiling, "but I expect I'll be pretty busy about that time — all of us will, if what Luddin figures comes true and the Comancheros show up this morning."

"You still have to eat. I could bring a little something to you —"

"Too risky for you. Besides, I want you and all of the women down under those wagons when trouble starts, and I want you to stay there. Probably going to be quite a chore keeping the children from getting hurt."

"We'll look out for them," Carla said with a shrug. "Maybe tonight, if things quiet down, you could come."

Shawn glanced toward the center of the camp. Deke Benjamin was hurrying toward him. Touching the brim of his hat, Starbuck nodded to the girl.

"Seems I'm needed," he said, turning away. "Thanks again for the invitation."

Leaving the wagons, he crossed to meet

the redhead. It was growing warm in the canyon and Benjamin's ruddy face had the shine of sweat on it.

"Found two cans of black powder," he said as he drew close. "Figure to plant it inside the mouth of the canyon, lay a powder string that I can set off at the right moment. Be a mighty fine welcome for Valdez and his bunch."

Starbuck grinned. "Will at that," he said, eyes shifting to the stockade where Davey Joe and Zeb Traxler were coming through the gate with three of the Comanchero women. "Just don't set it where the explosion will block us in."

"Aimed to keep it back a ways. Be mostly flash and dirt, but it'll account for a few of them renegades and make the rest do a bit of thinking."

"Need all the help we can get along those lines. Work down at that end coming along all right?"

"Same as done. Mayo's got a dozen or more of those fortifications made up, all fixed like you wanted. Finch and that fellow Kane went after Jed Willard's body. Buried it at the foot of the south wall."

"Dagget's still standing his watch —"

"Seen him up there about five minutes ago."

Starbuck nodded in satisfaction. "Everything's set at this end. Guess we're ready as we can get."

"Will be for sure, soon as I stash this blasting powder," Benjamin said, and hurried off.

Shawn, attention again on the two Texans and the Comanchero women coming from one of the brush shelters, angled across the open ground toward them, question in his eyes. Any sort of familiarity with the prisoners could lead to trouble.

Traxler read his disapproval. "Was letting them get some grub," he explained. "All of them was bellyaching to Davey Joe about being hungry. He asked was it all right and I said it was — long as I went along. . . . Left Orvy to watch the gate."

Starbuck looked closely at the women. They had made sling baskets of their skirts, filled them with ears of corn, slabs of dried meat, and small, yellow melons. One had hung a skin canteen over her shoulder. They returned Shawn's scrutiny with arrogant indifference.

Davey Joe, preceding them by a couple of strides, pointed to the youngest of the trio, a wide grin on his face. The girl had lifted her full skirt considerably higher than the others and her legs were revealed from mid-thigh down.

"Now, ain't that a pretty sight?" he declared, admiringly.

Starbuck glanced at Traxler. "You make sure they didn't pick up something that could be used as a weapon?"

"Watched sharp," the scout assured him. "Both of us. Ain't nothing there but vittles." He swung his angry eyes to the younger man. "And you keep your mind on your business, Davey Joe! This ain't no time for foolishness."

"Something like that is my business," the young Texan answered, his grin becoming even broader.

Shawn stepped aside, watched the Comanchero women file back into the stockade, Davey Joe, now following, waited until he saw Orvy knot the rope that held the gate in place, and then turned to the scout.

"Next time it'll be a better idea for one of us to carry grub to them. I don't figure they can be trusted."

"Whatever you say, Gen'ral," Traxler murmured in a slightly aggrieved tone. "There anything more that needs doing?"

"Guess we're ready for them."

The scout rubbed at his neck. "Can't come too soon to suit me. Sure don't favor standing around," he said as they moved off toward the mouth of the canyon.

Kane and Adam Finch, rifles cradled in their arms, strolled up, the latter mopping his face with a red bandanna.

"Ought to be showing up," he said, sweeping the canyon's rim with his eyes. "What was them Mex women doing running loose?"

"Weren't loose," Traxler snapped. "Me and Davey Joe was watching them close. Had to let them get some grub. Even Comancheros have to eat."

"Can starve far as I care," Finch growled.

"Was none of that bunch in the stockade women, reckon I'd feel the same. Can't blame them because their menfolk are stinking outlaws. . . . Starbuck, we setting up regular sentry posts?"

"Might be a good idea," Shawn said. "Somebody ought to spell Dagget."

"How about putting a man at the head of the canyon? Good place up there by them big rocks."

"Take him too long to get down here when he got Valdez spotted. Would mean riding the whole length of the canyon."

"Yeh, reckon you're right. Want me to go swap with Dagget?"

"Expect he'd appreciate it —"

"No need," Jim Kane cut in quietly. "He's coming this way — fast. Reckon he's seen them Comancheros."

Orvy Clark caught Davey Joe's big wink as he followed the Comanchero women into the stockade, knew immediately what his friend had in mind. Davey Joe was aiming to somehow corner the Mex girl who was showing off her legs and have himself a time.

Orvy shook his head sadly. He wished again he could be like Davey Joe. He really got around plenty and did just about what he took a notion to do — and the hell with what anybody else thought.

That was the way a man ought to be — independent, doing his own thinking, and getting what he wanted. He reckoned he'd never be like Davey Joe; it just didn't come natural. When it came to answering folks, Davey Joe had a right quick tongue, along with a real snappy line he always handed the girls which, according to Davey Joe, always got him what he was after.

Turning, Orvy looked through the brush and post palings of the stockade face. Davey Joe was standing near the girl. He'd lent her his knife and she was using it to cut off chunks of the dried meat they'd toted in. He was smiling, and although Orvy couldn't see the girl's face, he bet she was smiling, too. Davey Joe could talk a little of their jabber — enough, he always said, to get the job done.

That's just what he was doing right then — getting the job done. More than likely they'd both disappear pretty quick, and then Davey Joe'd have another long tale to tell.

Orvy sighed, turned back around, faced the upper end of the canyon where Starbuck and the others had gathered. His folks had warned him a-plenty about running around with Davey Joe, him being wild like he was. They'd even said that someday he'd likely get himself killed if he didn't watch his p's and q's.

Maybe so, but it sure would be grand if he could have a little of that fun Davey Joe was always spouting off about.

15

Starbuck, with Kane and Zeb Traxler at his shoulders, hurried forward to meet the squatly built Dagget. The man was hunched low over his horse as he raced recklessly down the slope into the mouth of the canyon, shouting his warning as he came, despite Shawn's earlier cautioning.

"The dang fool!" Traxler said. "If he's going to yell like that, we ain't keeping our hideout in here no surprise from the Comancheros for long."

Dagget rushed up, pulled his horse to a sliding halt. "They're coming!" he yelled, and pointed toward the west.

"How far?" Shawn asked, tautly.

"Half mile, maybe less."

"Big party of them?"

"Lot of dust, but I'd say thirty or forty —"

"You figure they seen you?" Traxler wondered.

"Nope, don't think so."

"Well, was they any closer they'd sure'n hell heard you," the old scout grumbled, and faced Starbuck. "Where you want us?"

"Pick yourself a barricade. Idea is to stop them when they start to ride in — more damage we can do right at the first, better off we'll be. Remember Deke Benjamin's set a powder charge. Let him fire it before you open up."

"Where'd he put it?" Traxler asked, thumbing cartridges from his belt and stuffing them into a pocket where they would be more quickly available.

"Across the mouth of the canyon. . . . Let's spread the word."

Dagget spurred off toward the corrals to leave his horse, sounding the alarm as he went. Kane and Traxler separated, the gunman moving forward, the scout dropping back. Shawn, hurriedly passing him by, reached the wagons, voiced a warning, and then crossed to the stockade.

"They're coming," he called to Orvy. "You and Davey Joe keep that bunch quiet —"

From the other side of the fence Davey Joe shouted: "How long I have to stay in here?"

"Until after the shooting starts. Expect you to come out and give us a hand then.

Orvy, best you keep on guarding that gate. Don't want any of them running loose."

"Yes, sir," the younger man answered.

Wheeling, Starbuck headed back for the upper end of the sink. The Comancheros should be drawing near by that moment and it was necessary that every man be in place before the outlaws reached the entrance. The one possibility of a hitch lay in Valdez and his men approaching the canyon from the side, and looking down into its depth, note the absence of activity.

He drew abreast the first bulwark. Traxler squatted on his heels between the arrangement of two large rocks placed little more than shoulder's width apart. The scout grinned, waved.

"Let 'em come!" he said.

Finch and Mayo occupied the next, some twenty feet to the right and farther on. Both nodded, indicating their readiness. He continued on to the succeeding barricade, one constructed of several logs and smaller rocks within which Tom Luddin and his younger son crouched. Beyond them in the staggered line was the wagon-train man's other son and Abe Wagner.

"All of you — keep down low," he called as he passed.

Mort Dagget and Lawton, the one remaining member of the train, knelt side by side, rifles ready, in the fortification a short distance farther on. Both nodded to him soberly.

"Luck —" he said in reply.

Jim Kane and Benjamin were in the last and largest of the arrangements, which was also the one nearest to the entrance. As Shawn came up, both men shifted to the side, made room for him. Drawing his pistol he laid it on the flat surface of the rock before him and glanced toward the rim.

"No sign?"

Benjamin shook his head. "Not yet," he said, and pointed to a narrow black line on the dry ground running from the edge of the barricade to the mouth of the canyon.

"Got my welcoming committee all ready," he said with a hard grin. "I just strike a lucifer, drop it, and up she goes."

"You're figuring to let them ride in to where they're almost on it, I expect," Shawn said. "Be a shame to wait too long, let them trample the fuse and —"

"Done this plenty of times before," Benjamin said stiffly. "Ain't no greenhorn at it."

"Didn't think you were," Starbuck replied, and fixed his attention on a pall of dust beyond the south rim.

A frown pulled at his features. He'd hoped

the Comancheros would make a direct approach from the east; if they came up onto the canyon from the south, there was greater chance of their becoming suspicious when they saw no signs of life.

Twisting about, he faced the other barricades. "To the south!" he called, keeping his voice as low as possible. "Stay low and out of sight."

Kane read his worry. He brushed at the sweat on his face as he said, "Trail maybe swings around the hill —"

"What I'm hoping," Starbuck said. He continued to watch the dust cloud, thickening now as the Valdez party drew nearer.

The minutes dragged by, filled with mounting heat and tension. Shortly the pall seemed to grow thinner. Shawn breathed easier; apparently the trail did cut to the east — and then he realized that was wrong, that the Comancheros were moving through a rocky area where there was little loose dirt to create a dust cloud.

"There they are," Deke Benjamin said in a strained voice.

Starbuck made no comment. The outlaws were breaking into view along the rim, riding in single file toward the mouth of the canyon. In the harsh desert sunlight their features looked almost black beneath the wide, rolled brims of their high peaked sombreros. They appeared to notice nothing out of the ordinary in the canyon below them, simply rode steadily on, heads down.

"Cuidado! Americanos aqui!"

The yell came from the stockade, was followed immediately by a gunshot. An oath ripped from Starbuck's lips. He wheeled about. The captive outlaws were pouring out of the gate and into the open, shouting as they came. Orvy Harrison lay face down in the dirt. He could not see Davey Joe. Somehow the prisoners had managed to overcome him, take Orvy by surprise, and escape.

Gunfire broke out from the barricade nearest the stockade — one manned by Zeb Traxler, and then Mayo and Finch from nearby began to trigger their weapons. The onrushing prisoners wilted. Several went down. The man in the lead, a pistol in his hand, sagged to his knees, emptying his gun at Traxler as he fell forward.

Shots were now crackling along the rim of the canyon and geysers of dust were spurting from its floor. The men in the barricades opened up with a return fire and for several minutes the air was filled with the blast of rifles and pistols, the smell of burned powder and swirling clouds of smoke and dust.

Gradually the shooting died. The line of heads barely visible along the upper edge of the sink disappeared. Starbuck, keeping down, turned grimly to the other bulwarks.

"Stay where you are!" he yelled. There no longer was a need for silence. "They'll be circling. . . . How bad is it down there?"

The word came up the line quickly. Traxler had been hit, looked to be dead. The same went for Orvy. They could see a knife — Davey Joe's big Bowie — sticking out of his back. Nobody could see Davey Joe. He was still inside the stockade, but he probably was dead, too. It was his gun the outlaw was using when he came charging out of the gate.

Starbuck swore. Three men dead and the real fight had yet to begin. The casualties they'd sustained could be chalked up to a surprise move — due to somebody's carelessness — within the camp. Valdez could take no credit for them, but that was small consolation. And the pendulum was swinging to the Comancheros; counting Jed Willard, the posse was now four guns less.

"Like to know what the hell was going on down there," Benjamin muttered, eyes narrowed on the stockade. "Somebody was laying down on the job."

Jim Kane shrugged. "Don't see as it matters, now."

"Would if this were the army! I'd see to it that whoever was responsible was brought up on charges —"

"You can't hang a dead man," Kane cut in, drily.

A quarter hour dragged by, slowly passing minutes filled with mounting heat, the fading of gunsmoke, the settling of dust, and tension. A horse in one of the corrals began to buck and pitch as something irritated him — likely one of the big, vicious flies that swarmed around the camp.

There was no more commotion at the stockade and the half-a-dozen bodies sprawled in front of the gate remained motionless. There could be two or three men yet inside, along with the women who had not participated in the break, but they evidently had no wish to try for an escape. They would wait instead for their friends to free them.

"Up — behind us," Kane said.

Shawn came about. Men were appearing now on the rim beyond the camp. Moments later others came into view along the north, and then to the east. As he had expected,

Valdez was ringing the canyon with his followers.

"Can figure on them rushing us now," Deke Benjamin said.

The army man's voice was filled with excitement. He moved forward, squatted, hand digging into a pocket for matches. Starbuck threw a glance to the opening in the steep walls. A thin dust cloud was moving up from the outside, the dim shapes of a dozen or so riders barely visible through it.

"I can't see so good from down here," the redhead said, looking over his shoulder at Starbuck. "You give me the word."

Shawn nodded, turned his attention again to the blur at the entrance of the canyon. The party was becoming more distinct. He guessed the riders would come in as close as possible, form ranks, and then charge.

"Light your match," he said. "When I say *now,* touch off the fuse string."

He heard Benjamin scrape the sulphur-tipped sliver of wood into flame and kept his eyes on the Comancheros. A tight hush gripped the canyon, and the only movement visible was a pair of white-winged doves flying an erratic course overhead. It was as if the universe had paused, was awaiting the outcome of the pending moments.

A half-a-dozen horses, heads bobbing up and down as they walked, appeared suddenly in the opening. A like number crowded in close behind them. All halted, the men astride seemingly preparing themselves. A yell went up.

"Now!" Starbuck snapped.

Deke Benjamin moved slightly. A burst of sizzling flame shot up in front of the barricade, raced forward to meet the oncoming riders. Abruptly a sheet of fire erupted. Dust, smoke, and screams of pain filled that end of the canyon, mingling with the thundering echoes.

Guns began to crack spitefully along the rim. Deke Benjamin leaped to his feet, began levering bullets into the swirling confusion.

"Stay down!" Starbuck yelled, frantically trying to reach the man and drag him back, but the redhead pulled away.

And then he paused, half turned, a frown on his sweaty, dust-covered face. "Hell — I've been shot," he said in a puzzled sort of voice, and fell heavily.

On hands and knees Kane moved to the man, bent over him. After a bit he shrugged.

"Dead —"

Starbuck stirred wearily. Deke Benjamin had wasted himself. In the heat of excitement he had, contrary to his military training and experience, thoughtlessly exposed himself and paid the full price.

"Got seven of them," Kane said in an emotionless tone.

Shawn transferred his attention to the mouth of the canyon. Several bodies lay visible in the thinning dust along with four dead horses. Beyond them the remainder of the charging force was beating a hurried retreat.

"Reckon they won't be trying that again," Kane continued, picking up Benjamin's rifle and beginning to reload it.

Starbuck nodded. The Comancheros had failed both from above and below to force an entry. Likely Valdez would sit back now, rely on sniping and hope to starve them out. He could not know, of course, that help for the party holding the camp, in the form of the Federalista cavalry, was on the way.

"Nothing to do now but wait," he said. "Be no chore holding that bunch off until the soldiers get here. We've proved that to them — and ourselves."

Kane, finished with restocking the rifle, paused, his flat eyes on the east rim of the big arroyo.

"Guess we can forget that," he said in his laconic way.

Shawn raised his glance. Disappointment flooded through him. A man, hands tied behind him, a rope about his neck, was standing in full view of all in the canyon below.

It was Ben.

16

A heavy sigh escaped Shawn Starbuck. He brushed agitatedly at his jaw. The possibility of aid from the Mexican army was gone. If he and the remaining Texans were to get the Luddin party safely back to the border, they would have to do it on their own.

And then a surge of self-realization washed over him, thrusting aside the problem. That was Ben up there! Ben, the brother for whom he'd searched so long — the reason why he was here, deep in the hostile Chihuahua Desert literally fighting for his life.

Reaching down he took the pair of well-worn army field-glasses from the case lying beside Deke Benjamin's body, and holding them to his eyes, focused them on the figure silhouetted on the rim.

Hatless, dark hair awry, clothing torn, and with blood smears on his face, it was evident Ben had been handled roughly. He looked much as Shawn thought he would; a man solidly built, with the square, patient features of their pa, and the thick, powerful shoulders that reflected his strength.

As Starbuck watched, someone from behind and below jerked on the rope. Ben staggered back, dropped from sight. Shawn lowered the glasses, slipped them back into their imitation leather case.

"Your brother?"

At Kane's question Starbuck nodded. "First look I've had of him since he left home — thirteen years ago."

"Long time," Kane murmured. "He in bad shape?"

"Been worked over plenty, I'd say, but didn't seem hurt too much."

Kane reached into his shirt pocket. Bringing out the makings, he began to roll a cigarette. "Valdez knew what he was doing — standing your brother up there like that so's we could all see him. Wanted us to know the Federalistas wouldn't be coming. . . . Probably figures we'll give in now."

"Tightens the noose a bit for sure," Shawn admitted, glancing back into the canyon. The men were all holding their places, respectful of the guns they knew were still looking down on them from the rim above.

"What're we doing next — you figured that out yet?"

"Sit tight 'til dark. By then maybe —"

A sudden blast of gunfire cut into his words. Bullets smashed into the barricades, thudding hollowly as they buried themselves into wood, spanging shrilly into space when they glanced off rock.

"Going to try again, seems," Kane said, flipping away his cigarette. Taking up a rifle, he rested it upon the edge of the barricade, and sighting along its barrel, began to methodically pump shots at the puffs of smoke along the rim.

"Ain't much chance of hitting one of them jaspers," he said, "scrunched down behind the rocks the way they are, but we sure better let them know we're still alive and kicking."

Starbuck agreed, and keeping an eye on the entrance to the canyon in the event a second attempt to storm their defenses was made, he added his fire to that of Jim Kane.

Elsewhere other members of the posse and the men of the wagon train were throwing up a steady return. If the renewed assault on the part of the Comancheros, coming shortly after they had let it be known Ben's efforts to get help had failed, was meant to be a testing maneuver designed to determine if the trapped Tejanos were ready to surrender, they had gotten their answer quickly and emphatically.

A yell from above broke through the hammering of guns. A figure rose stiffly among the rocks, lurched forward, plunged over the edge of the canyon to the floor below. One of the men had gotten in a lucky shot. The Comanchero guns fell silent almost immediately.

Starbuck flipped open the loading gate of his pistol, refilled the cylinder, turned to the rifle he had used, replenished its magazine.

"What do you reckon they'll try next?" Kane wondered, servicing his own weapons.

"Maybe nothing. Valdez knows all he has to do is wait us out. We'll be needing water in a few days. Grub, too, and with women and kids to think of, that can be a problem."

"Then I guess we sure better be coming up with an idea —"

"Think I have," Shawn said, and turned about to face the men crouching in the nearest barricade. "Everybody sit tight. When night comes, move up here for a talk. . . . Pass the word along."

Talk!

John Mayo, with Adam Finch hunched beside him in their shelter, swore angrily. When you got right down to it, talk was what got them in the jam they were in —

talk and voting and letting the wrong man take over the posse.

"What kind of a mess you figure he's aiming to get us into now?" he demanded, shaking his head at his partner.

Finch shrugged. "Expect he knows what he's doing. Can't blame him if them Comancheros grabbed his brother and kept him from finding the soldiers."

"Was a damn fool thing to gamble on in the first place! If it'd been me calling the shots, we'd a been out of here and half way to the border by now."

"Maybe —"

"Maybe, hell! We ain't done nothing but back ourselves into a pocket doing what he wanted."

"We'd been no better off out there on the flats with Valdez and his bunch picking us off one at a time when they caught up with us. Leastwise in here they can't do that."

"What do you mean they can't? By God, we've got three men dead not counting Willard, and there's probably —"

"Can't blame Starbuck for that, either. If they'd been looking out for themselves like he told them, they'd be alive and kicking right now."

"Still mighty dead," the lawman muttered stubbornly, changing his position to where he could see the barricade that Starbuck, Deke Benjamin, and the gunslinger, Jim Kane, were manning.

"If we're holding a meeting, it'd best be down at the wagons. Expect them women and their kids are plenty scared by now."

"Probably wants it up here so's we can keep an eye out for those Comancheros trying to charge us again. Dark works both ways — for them same as us."

"If it was me, I'd put a couple of guards out there —"

"Two men couldn't hold back a rush like they made. Fact is, it was the gunpowder that Deke Benjamin planted that stopped them — and there's none left. Expect the only thing that's keeping Valdez from making another try is that he doesn't know that."

Mayo stirred impatiently. No matter what he mentioned, Finch came up with some argument against it. That Starbuck had really won over the whole bunch of them, pulling them away from him — a lawman with a world of experience — and wheedling them into doing what he wanted.

Well, they saw now where listening to him had got them — bottled up in a box canyon with a bunch of sodbusters and their women and kids on their hands — and no way out!

He'd bet they'd all think twice about

backing Starbuck if they had it to do over again! This time they'd listen to him, a man who'd been down the road a far piece met up with the same kind of a deal a few dozen times and come out on top.

Hell, there just wasn't no substitute for experience, they all knew that, and if they'd been thinking straight and not got all fired up by that big hard case and his way of talking, they would have remembered it. . . . Sure, he'd got a mite old, and maybe he just didn't react fast like once he did, but he was still a straight thinker, and that's what really counted — thinking straight and then having the guts to go ahead and do what was necessary.

Mayo reckoned it was going to be up to him to get them all out of the pickle they were in — the folks of the wagon train and the posse — what was left of it. He'd put his mind to it, and when they got together after dark, he'd push this Starbuck aside and take charge, and tell them all what had to be done.

A sudden crackle of gunshots brought the lawman about. At the lower end of the canyon, beyond the wagons, two Comancheros were clinging frantically to ropes that had been dropped over the lip of the wall. Evidently Valdez was making a stab at getting men into the camp by that route.

As Mayo watched, both of the outlaws, blood staining their loose cotton shirts where bullets had smashed into their bodies, released their grip and fell heavily onto the jagged rubble of rocks below.

"They won't be trying that again," Finch said. "Must've figured we wouldn't be watching — or maybe couldn't shoot so good."

"Be different after it's dark," Mayo said. "They'll be able to throw a dozen ropes over the side and we won't be able to see them doing it."

Adam Finch stared at the lawman. "Sounds like you're sort of glad of that!"

Mayo shook his head hurriedly. "No, course I ain't. Just pointing it out."

17

Long before night fell, the Comancheros encircling the canyon had built fires along the rim, and when the men of the posse and wagon train gathered at Shawn's summons to discuss their escape, they did so beneath a pale yellow glow that filled the darkness.

Starbuck, worried about Ben's fate as well as the people he now felt responsibility for, had first sent word to the women, instructing them to stay close to the wagons and keep close watch on the wall behind them where earlier the Comancheros had attempted a descent.

It was the only part of the canyon where such could be effected, and since it was necessary the men all gather near the entrance and be in position should another rush take place, the chore fell to the women. They were to sound a warning by firing off a shotgun if they saw the start of another try.

"Ought to take care of the dead first," Mort Dagget said as they gathered around Starbuck. "Just ain't decent letting them lay out there."

"We'll get to that," Shawn replied. "Important we think about the living right now."

"For a fact," Kane murmured. "They sure ain't going nowheres."

"Well, you got a scheme?" Mayo asked, his voice brusque. "Has to be better'n the ones you've had! We've got five men killed — can't affort to lose no more."

Starbuck studied the old lawman in the pale light. They would not have complete darkness in their favor as they'd had the previous night; the overcast had cleared away, and while there was still no moon, the stars were out and glittering brightly.

"Like to say something before this here gets started," Luddin said, rubbing his big hands together. "Goes without telling how much we're obliged to you men for coming after us, trying to help —"

"And we're mighty sorry about the ones that've got themselves killed," Wagner added. "Only wish there was some way we could show you how much —"

"Thanks ain't what we're needing," Mayo snapped. "What we're needing is a way out of this trap he's got us into."

Finch swore impatiently. "Maybe if you'd give Starbuck a chance to talk —"

"Letting him talk's got us in one hell of a hole," the lawman continued, "one we ain't likely to crawl out of."

"No more his fault than ours," Finch countered.

"Well, this damned yammering ain't getting nothing done," Dagget said tiredly. "Why don't we all just simmer down and see what he's got to say?"

Shawn smiled tautly. He'd listened to the words thrown back and forth, and it was on the tip of his tongue to tell John Mayo to take over, and welcome, thus release him and make it possible for him to go to Ben's aid — or at least try. Alone, he was fairly certain he could work his way up to where his brother was being held captive, and when the outlaws quieted down for the night, free him. But his obligation to the men of the posse, the men, women and children of —

"What've you got in mind?" Dagget's words cut into Starbuck's thoughts. "I reckon everybody's ready to listen now," he added, looking pointedly at Mayo.

"Just this," Shawn said. "You can all see there's no chance of help coming from the Federalistas. Means we'll have to get out of here on our own —"

"Which we sure would've been if you all had listened to me," Mayo declared.

"And we'd all been dead or prisoners of Valdez and his bunch of pistoleros if we had," Kane said.

"You ain't sure of that! We could've —"

"Goddammit, Marshal — shut up!" Dagget exploded, suddenly out of patience. "I want to hear the man. So do the rest."

The lawman stared at Mort Dagget, jaw sagging slightly. The onetime coach driver's forcefulness seemingly took him by surprise.

"All that counts for nothing now," Starbuck went on. "I figure we've got one chance to get Luddin and his people out of here — do it the way we got in."

Adam Finch frowned. "You mean get rid of the guards, slip by?"

"Exactly. Won't be any harder going out than coming in. Probably four, maybe a half-a-dozen Comancheros posted at the mouth of the canyon. We take care of them same way we did the others. Once that's done we'll have Luddin take his party through and head for the border."

"Wagons are going to make a lot of racket," Wagner said. "And the way sound carries —"

"Forget them. You'll be riding horseback.

Means you'll leave behind everything you don't absolutely need."

"What about the young 'uns?" Dagget asked. "Going to be hard to keep them quiet."

"They can put gags on them — long enough to get clear of the canyon."

Luddin glanced at Wagner and the third member of the train, Tait Lawton. Both nodded. Mayo shook his head.

"Seems to me you're forgetting something," he said. "Was you telling us we'd not get far when I wanted to do just what you're proposing. You claimed the Comancheros would follow us, catch up —"

"They won't know they're gone," Starbuck replied.

"Won't know? Hell, when morning comes and Valdez and his crowd looks down here and sees the place deserted —"

"We'll be here," Shawn said quietly. "Only the wagon train party will be gone. We'll be covering for them while they get away."

There was a long pause. Up on the rim one of the outlaws was singing in a wild voice, accompanied by many hands clapping in rhythm. The sound seemed remote, hollow.

"We get them out, but we stay," Kane said slowly. "That the deal?"

Starbuck smiled grimly. "What I mean. We keep moving around a little, maybe make use of some of the women's dresses and the like, I figure Valdez and his bunch won't ever get wise."

"Wouldn't hurt none, I suppose, to sort of prop up the dead, make it look like they're standing watch," Lawton suggested. "I mean it wouldn't be no disrespect."

"Not at a time like this," Finch agreed.

"Then what happens to us?" Mayo asked, shrugging. "We just keep setting here hoping for help to show up — drop down from heaven, maybe?"

"Luddin could run into the army on the way back," Starbuck explained, "but we won't plan on it. All we need to do is fool Valdez for one day. That'll give Luddin and his people time to get far enough along to where they'll be safe. Then when dark comes — that'll be tomorrow night — we'll pull out."

"Ought to work," Dagget said promptly.

"Maybe." John Mayo shook his head. "You're all overlooking something. Them guards you're figuring on putting out of business. Come morning they're going to be found. That'll tell Valdez mighty quick there's something haywire."

"He's right," Finch said. "Could make

Valdez suspicious — maybe send out riders for a look around."

"Be morning by then," Shawn said, "and I'm depending on Luddin having his party a long way from here."

"Still be tracks —"

"Realize that, but with a six or eight hour start everything'll be favoring them."

"Once we're out of here," Wagner said, "you can bank on us moving right smart. Only thing that might slow us down would be one of the horses going lame."

"Your womenfolk ride?" Dagget asked.

"They ain't no great shakes at it, but they all know how. Won't be nothing to worry about there."

"Still ain't said what we'll be doing about them dead guards," Mayo persisted.

"Don't intend for them to be found," Shawn said. "We'll carry them down here — and we won't leave any sign as to what happened. Then we start hoping the men who come to take their place in the morning will figure they just went on back to camp a little ahead of time and not think much about it. . . . Anyway, we can't expect to have it all the way we want it."

"That's for damned sure," Kane agreed.

Starbuck glanced around at the men. "That's the best I can come up with. If anybody else's got an idea or a suggestion, let's hear it."

There was no response. Tom Luddin bobbed. "Good enough. When you want us to start getting ready?"

"Now," Starbuck said flatly. "Sooner you're out of here, the more ground you will have covered by daylight. Get back to your women, tell them what the deal is. We'll fix you up with the saddle horses you'll have to have."

"Be needing pack animals, too —"

"They'll slow you down too much. You'll be traveling light, and you can spread among your people what you do have to carry. . . . You be ready to pull out in an hour?"

"Can — and will," the wagon-train man said, and beckoning to the others of his party, moved hurriedly off into the night.

Adam Finch, crouched low, halted beside a large rock at the canyon's entrance. Directly across, although he could neither see nor hear the man, Kane would be following a similar procedure. They had been directed by Starbuck to work in as close as possible, get the guards located so that no time would be lost when the moment came to remove them.

Almost at once, he caught sight of the Comancheros on his side; two of them crouched by a low fire just at the edge of the opening. They would be the only ones, he reasoned, since they were placed so as to block the path of anyone attempting to leave, but he had to be sure. After that he was to pull back. All Starbuck wanted was to know where the outlaws were stationed; he'd made it clear that he and Kane were not to move in regardless of how good an opportunity was presented, until the word was given.

Leaning against the cool surface of the boulder, Adam Finch allowed himself to rest. Ten years ago, if someone had suggested he would find himself one night, deep in the Mexican desert, hunched in the darkness awaiting word to kill another human being, he would have told them they were ready for the insane asylum.

But things were different then. He'd been an important man in an important New York city — a government official, in fact, with dozens at his beck and call and each anxious to do his bidding.

He'd had a family then, too — three fine boys, two beautiful daughters, and a wife that made him proud and stirred him deeply each time he looked at her. Fifteen years of marriage lay behind them; fifteen happy, prosperous years during which he had grown in stature and prominence.

And then had come Mason Zule, a man with a vast fortune and the mighty power of greatly respected ancestry, who had a plan that would lead to the Governor's mansion, possibly even higher in the political echelon.

He was also a person of excessive charm and most winning ways, and Adam Finch — in those days he was Adam Leigh — had gone along with his scheme, placing complete faith and trust in this individual of consequence who had taken such interest in him.

Disaster had come quickly. A matter of bribery, of missing funds, of deepest intrigue, all beyond Adam's knowledge. To Zule it had been a lark, a rich man's whimsy, never mind that it had brought disgrace and finality to a promising career as well as the destruction of a family; to him it had been diversion, fun.

Adam Finch had not borne it well. On the day after he buried his wife, victim of a weak heart that failed in its efforts to withstand the shame, he'd sent his children, together with a satchel containing all the money he possessed, except for pocket change, to live with a sister in Connecticut, and acquiring a revolver, he sought out Mason Zule and shot him dead.

With the police only hours behind him, he caught a ride on a train headed west, stayed with it until there were no longer any rails. There he purchased a horse and continued on, eventually losing himself in the broad state of Texas, now recovering from the inroads of war and growing steadily. Eventually he wandered into the settlement of Sabine Springs, and finding its stagnation to his liking, settled there.

He heard no more from New York, nor from his children whom he feared to contact. They would be almost grown, he often thought, and probably had small recollection of him — which was just as well. They would not be proud that their father was a murderer.

He'd made a mistake, he supposed, handling the situation as he had, but at the time he saw no other course. Zule had caused the death of his wife, ruined him politically by his chicanery, and in so doing had destroyed him. Zule deserved to die — and he did. But it all washed out as cold-blooded murder and placed him outside the law. He had never found it in himself to be sorry for the act; he only regretted that it had cut him off from his sons and daughters.

. . . Someday, perhaps, he would see them again. Years had a way of blurring the records, and men's memories of events faded. When he felt that time had come he would —

An owl hooted softly somewhere back in the canyon. Finch straightened, pulled himself away from the rock. It was the signal. Starbuck and the others were coming. Turning about, he gave a quiet reply.

18

"How many of them up there?" Starbuck asked, studying the slope rising before him.

"Two," Jim Kane answered as they hunched side by side in the darkness. "One setting there by them high rocks. Another'n a bit beyond. Don't think there's any more'n that but I ain't for certain."

"Likely only two. That's what Finch spotted on the other side. Means we're dealing with four of them."

Half turning, he glanced over his shoulder. John Mayo had the Luddin party strung out behind him, each member leading a horse. They were drawn up beside the last barricade awaiting the sign to move out. All had been instructed to walk their mount through the mouth of the canyon and continue to do so for another quarter mile before going to the saddle. Such would give them a much lower profile and lessen the possibility of becoming outlined against the night.

"You want me to get them guards?"

At Kane's low-voiced question Starbuck came back around. "We'll both do it. Dagget and Finch are looking after the other pair."

"Suits me," Kane murmured. "I'll go for the one by the rocks. You get that'n back of him."

Shawn glanced again at Mayo. The lawman had wanted to be one of those to clear the way. He had arranged to trade jobs with Mort Dagget. He had changed their plans. Climbing about in the rocks and brush, he knew from previous experience, required a much younger man. He did not tell the old lawman such in so many words, however, had simply made it appear that Mayo's services in leading the Luddin party through the mouth of the canyon when the signal was given, and doing it quickly and silently, was all important.

Turning his face to the opposite side of the deep wash, Shawn made a quiet, clicking sound. "Let's go," he murmured, and began to work his way up the grade.

Kane moved with him for a short distance and then began to fade left. Starbuck continued, carefully picking his way toward the mound where the second sentry had been posted.

From across the entrance, the thump and rattle of a rock, displaced and tumbling to a lower level, reached Starbuck. He halted, alarm rising within him. Finch or Dagget had made a misstep. It could alert the Comancheros. Taut, he waited, eyes searching the shadowy slopes, the one ahead of him and its counterpart across the way, ears straining to catch the sounds of movement.

Off to his left a figure rose from the darkness by a mound of rocks, a tall, hulking shape topped by a large, high-peaked hat.

"Quien es?"

The words had scarcely been voiced when a second figure appeared, closed in swiftly and silently. The man in the tall hat buckled, sank into the blackness, and then all was quiet.

Starbuck moved on, still pointing for the higher part of the slope. He covered a half-a-dozen steps, slowed as the dry rasp of clothing dragging against the stiff saltbush warned him of another's presence. Hand tightening about his knife, he again waited.

Shortly the second Comanchero came into view. He was working his way down slope. Evidently he had heard his partner call out and then fall silent and was now going to investigate. Following his present course, he would walk straight into Jim Kane.

Shawn crouched, knife poised, until the outlaw had drawn abreast, and then, cat-like, closed in. He could not afford to let the man cry out; he'd made such clear to Kane and the others as well. One yell and they likely would have the entire outlaw gang down on their backs.

He struck hard. The Comanchero gasped, began to fall. Starbuck caught his rifle in one hand to prevent its clattering onto the rocks, flung an arm around his waist, and lowered him to the ground. From the nearby shadows Jim Kane's voice came softly to him.

"Reckon that takes care of them two. We having us a squint at the other side?"

"Best we play it safe," Shawn said, and together resumed the climb to the crest of the slope.

As they reached there the clicking of an insect came to them from the opposite grade. Dagget and Finch had completed their chore, would now also press on to the summit rising before them and search for any further problems. Starbuck made his acknowledgment by echoing the clicking sound, and with Kane hunched beside him, crossed the flinty ridge and pulled up behind a thick clump of brush. The grade sliding down from the canyon's east side crest was considerably less rugged, and after a few minutes' careful scanning, he shook his head.

"Nobody out there — I'm sure of it," he said, looking back toward the head of the canyon. Small fires burned along its rim, but they did not extend farther east than those being maintained by the guards they had just overcome.

But Starbuck was of no mind to take any chances. The lives of all those in the Luddin party, as well as the posse members, depended upon him being right.

"I'm having a look around at the bottom of the slope," he said in a low whisper. "Wait here."

"Reckon I'd as soon side you," Kane answered.

They reached the foot of the grade without encountering anyone, and cutting to their left, dropped down into the sandy mouth of the canyon. Taking a final look around, reassuring himself that none of the outlaws from the camp above had for some reason roused and were coming to be with their friends, Shawn cupped a hand to his lips and gave the agreed upon signal to

John Mayo.

At once a faint rustling came from the edge of the wash. Kane's two pistols whipped up, leveled, their long barrels glinting dully in the half light. The voice of Mort Dagget reached them instantly.

"It's only us — Dagget and Finch."

Starbuck relaxed, swung his glance to the wall of darkness that marked the mouth of the canyon. A thread of anxiety was stirring through him. Mayo and the Luddin party should be moving up.

"Heard you hooting," Dagget said as he and Finch halted beside Kane and Shawn. "Figured everything was going all right."

"Won't be for long," Kane muttered, "unless they shake loose a bit."

"Them now —" Adam Finch said.

The old lawman was in the lead, taking slow, careful strides. Behind him came Tom Luddin, a pack strapped to his broad shoulders, horse plodding patiently at his heels.

The party drew alongside, men silent and grim, the women with tightset lips and averted eyes. Two of the children had strips across their mouths and both were squirming mightily in the arms of their mothers. The girl, Carla, paused as she passed Starbuck and smiled.

"Thank you —"

"Good luck," he replied, and watched the small cavalcade file by.

"Reckon we've done all we can for them," Dagget said as the last of the party faded into the night.

Shawn nodded. "All but keeping Valdez and his bunch tied up. . . . We better get back to those guards and lug them back to camp."

"You figured what we're doing with them?" Mayo asked.

"Prop them up in the barricades — like they were some of us."

"Got to hide those big hats they're wearing," Finch said. "Sure give it away if somebody up on the rim spots them."

They slipped off into the darkness, moving quietly as before, but not finding it necessary to double back over the slopes to reach the bodies of the outlaws. Kane, staying with Starbuck, returned the pair they had accounted for, while Dagget and Finch, accompanied by John Mayo, recovered the other two.

A time later, the Comancheros, minus their distinctive headgear, had been deposited variously in different barricades along the floor of the canyon. As an added touch, their rifles were laid across the tops of the shelters in full view, giving the impression of men being ready and waiting to fight at any opportunity. Earlier, the bodies of the posse members who had fallen had been brought in, wrapped in blankets, and placed beside the wagons. There was no inclination on the part of Starbuck and the others to make use of their comrade's bodies.

The chore of stationing the Comanchero guards disposed of, Shawn led the remaining members of the posse, a pitifully small handful numbering four, through the shadows edging the canyon to where the wagons were parked.

There they found a supply of food thoughtfully prepared for their use by the women, along with a large pot of coffee left simmering over the coals of a dying fire. Replenishing the flames, they gathered around, careful to expose themselves only briefly to the outlaws on the rim, and satisfied their hunger.

When the meal was over they continued to move about, bearing in mind the need to make the camp appear as little changed as possible in the coming daylight. To that end several dresses and like garments, left behind by the Luddin party, were draped about in partly hidden locations to further the belief.

"What about horses?" Mayo wondered.

"Be smart to get them saddled, and load what we're taking with us so's we won't lose any time tonight."

Finch voiced Starbuck's thoughts before he could speak. "Be taking a chance. Somebody up there on the rim might notice them standing around all ready to go. He might tell Valdez. He'd figure we were getting ready to make a run for it, for sure."

"And we ain't in no shape to stand off another one of his charges," Dagget commented.

"There'll be plenty of time after dark," Shawn said. "Best you all see to your ammunition. Be my guess that they'll open up on us again, soon as it's light — if only to remind us they've still got us bottled up."

"I'm ready," Dagget said, fingering his cartridge belt and pockets. He waited while the others checked their reserve, and then, "Where you want us to squat?"

"One man in each barricade — having a body in it with you will make it look like two doing the shooting. Want whichever one of you is best with a rifle to be at this end of the canyon. Be up to him to stop any of the Comancheros trying to come down on ropes again.

"Reckon that'll be me," Dagget said. "Got right good with a long gun when I was working for the stage-line people."

"Seems I recollect you was a driver," Mayo said, rubbing at his jaw.

"Done both — driving and riding shotgun."

"Your job then," Shawn said. "Rest of us'll string out to where we're covering the floor of the canyon." Pausing, he glanced to the east. "About an hour until first light. We best get settled."

Dagget yawned, stretched. "Too bad Davey Joe ain't around for this. Was all the time talking about the Alamo and wishing he'd been there. I reckon we got us the same kind of a deal right here."

"Only we'll be getting out of this one," Starbuck said. "All we've got to do is make Valdez think we're all here and strong as ever, until dark. No big problem doing that if we use our heads."

"Sure won't," John Mayo said briskly. "Just keep under cover and shoot every time you get a chance. A man tries right hard, he'll be able to pick himself off a few of them Comancheros — like they was turkeys."

Shawn smiled, nodded. The old lawman's antagonism seemed to be fading. It was a relief to see it.

"Think I'd better tell you this now, Captain," he said, facing the older man. "When we ride out, I won't be going all the way with you."

Mayo frowned. "Why not? You sure'n hell can't stay here."

"Intend to see what I can do about my brother. I figure there's a good chance I can slip into the Comanchero camp up there and cut him loose during the night."

"You'll be needing help," Jim Kane said at once. "Count me in on your figuring."

"Same goes for me," Finch added.

"Expect it goes for all of us," Mort Dagget declared. "We ain't about to let you try something like that all by yourself."

Starbuck smiled. "I'm obliged to all of you, but it's a job one man can do better alone. . . . Can talk about it later, however." It was steadily growing lighter, and he was anxious for the men to find their places.

"Sure," Dagget said, and turned to go. "Good luck to you all —"

The others echoed his sentiment, moved off, each heading for the barricade chosen to man. Shawn waited until all had stationed themselves and then crossed to one of the remaining bulwarks, one near the center of the canyon, and settled himself. . . . Nightfall would tell whether he — alone or otherwise — would be going after Ben.

19

A deep hush lay over the canyon. Far to the east, long fingers of yellow were beginning to break through the pearl glare, and off to the south, a scatter of high-riding clouds were changing from white to a pale rose. There were no signs of movement along the rim, not even a rising twist of smoke.

"Something's wrong —"

It was John Mayo's voice. Starbuck, hunched in his barricade, shifted his attention to that point. The lawman was barely visible as he crouched between his rock and log bulwark some fifty feet or so opposite, on the floor of the big sink. Jim Kane occupied the shelter nearest the mouth of the canyon. Between him and Shawn, positioned in the center, was Adam Finch. Dagget, the expert rifleman, had assumed post in the one nearest the camp, the same one Zeb Traxler was manning when a bullet cut him down.

"You see something?" Finch asked.

"Nope, it's just that it's too blamed quiet. They ought to be stirring around. . . . Could be they've pulled out."

"They're up there," Starbuck said, more to himself than the others.

Dagget yawned noisily. " 'Spect they're just sleeping late. . . . Mighty pretty sunrise. Going to be a fine day for dying — if that's how it turns out."

"Ain't never seen a good day for that," Mayo said gruffly.

Starbuck drew up suddenly. Movement along the rim at the end of the canyon had caught his continually probing gaze. Heads appeared briefly, cautiously, and then in the early light a half-a-dozen ropes snaked over the side, began to dangle against the steep wall.

"Dagget!" he called sharply.

The squat coach-driver and shotgun messenger swiveled about, followed Shawn's pointing finger.

"They're plain foolish!" he declared, bringing up his rifle. "I didn't figure they'd be dumb enough to try that again. . . . Captain, that there turkey shoot you was talking about is going to commence."

Abruptly gunshots broke out along the edge of the canyon as Valdez and his men

195

sought to lay down a covering fire for the ones chosen to attempt the descent. Bullets thudded into the logs, screamed off rocks, and drove into hard-baked soil as before, doing no damage.

Well protected within the barricades, Starbuck and the posse members waited. Shortly, four of the outlaws appeared. Flat on their bellies they worked their way over the edge of the rim. Each grasping a rope, they started a hurried descent. The shooting along the rim increased.

Dagget, resting his rifle upon one of the larger rocks, pressed off a shot. With the belch of smoke from its muzzle, the outlaw on the rope farthest to the left jolted, released his grip, and fell.

Bullets hammered furiously at the barricade in which Dagget crouched as the Comancheros concentrated their fire on him. He seemed not to notice, triggered a second shot. The man clinging to the rope at the opposite end from the first, yelled, his voice echoing throughout the canyon. For a long moment he hung on, and then he, too, plummeted to the rocks below.

"This here one's for a fellow I knowed, name of Trevison!" Dagget shouted, and fired for a third time.

The Comanchero dropped instantly, apparently having been drilled through the heart. It was like an execution, Shawn thought — little different from a firing squad. Valdez apparently recognized the futility of the attempt and the shooting along the rim diminished further.

"Here goes number four!" Mort Dagget yelled.

His first bullet brought a puff of dust from the leg of the man's breeches, a yell of pain from his lips. The second caused an arm to drop, hang limply at his side. The third smashed into his other leg. Starbuck swore. Dagget was deliberately torturing the outlaw; it was as if he were venting his hatred on the man. Shawn lifted his own rifle, took close aim on the helpless, dangling figure, and pressed off a shot. The Comanchero released his grip on the rope, fell.

"Who the hell done that?" Dagget demanded angrily.

"Me," Starbuck answered coldly. "No call for that kind of treatment."

"Hell, they ain't nothing but a murdering bunch of outlaws — and they'd do it to us."

"Maybe so, but that's not the point. If you have to kill a man, kill him — get it over with quick."

"To my way of thinking, they had it coming," Mayo said, taking up a defense for

Dagget. "Can think of some worse things they done to folks over in Texas."

"An eye for an eye, I always say," Dagget said.

"Good rule, I reckon," Starbuck responded, "if you want to set yourself down on the same level with them —"

"Fire! They're shooting fire arrows!" Adam Finch yelled.

At the man's warning cry, Starbuck swung his eyes again to the rim at the end of the canyon. A half-a-dozen shafts, blazing brightly, were arcing toward the wagons.

"Let them fall!" he shouted, fearing that Dagget, acting impulsively, might rush out with an idea in mind of saving the vehicles.

The first arrows fell short, and then getting the range, the Indians — probably renegade Apache or Comanche members of Valdez' gang — dropped several squarely on the arched canvas tops of the wagons.

The burning shafts, upright in the stiff fabric, stood like torches for a brief time, and then, suddenly, flames seemed to explode from within the vehicles and both became a seething mass of fire.

Through the thick smoke and bits of ash boiling upward, Starbuck watched for movement along the rim. Setting fire to the wagons could be a diversion on the Comanchero's part, one intended to draw their attention to that specific point.

A figure became definite through the haze. Shawn threw up his rifle, aimed hastily, squeezed the trigger. The outlaw staggered, fell back out of sight. The rest of the posse took it up and for a full ten minutes the canyon rocked with the blast of guns both from within and outside its walls.

Again Shawn puzzled over Valdez and his actions. Why would the Comanchero leader go to so much trouble when all he need do was sit tight, allow thirst and hunger to eventually break down and end the resistance of the Texas posse, and as far as he knew, the wagon-train people. It had cost him several men.

And again it occurred to Starbuck that Valdez could simply be testing them, perhaps doing so at intervals, trying to assess the will of the trapped party. Too, in setting fire to the wagons, he could have thought such would cause several of the men to expose themselves in an effort to extinguish the flames and make it easy for his marksmen to shoot them down. If so, he had been disappointed; his guns so far had found no target except for the redhead, Deke Benjamin.

The shooting died entirely and there was

only the sound of the crackling flames, the occasional nicker of a frightened horse, and the pungent smell of burning wood and other items as the vehicles and their contents were consumed.

Shawn glanced at the sun, a round, red disc through the thick haze of black smoke now drifting slowly down the canyon. It was well above the horizon, but still hours short of midday, much less from setting. Luddin and the others would be miles away by that moment, unless something unforeseen had occurred, and noon would find them safely beyond the reach of the outlaws. But that meant little to him and the posse, as far as personal salvation was concerned; no escape was possible for them until after dark.

There was movement within the stockade where the remaining Comanchero prisoners were being held. They would be feeling the heat from the surging flames of the wagons, he guessed, were perhaps nervously considering the probability of the fire spreading to their own flimsy shelters and were entertaining thoughts of breaking out.

There was no danger to them, and aiming his rifle he fired a half-a-dozen bullets over the heads of the figures moving about in the dimness.

Dagget, considerably nearer to the stockade, spoke up immediately. "What is it? They trying to bust out?"

"Only letting them know we're keeping an eye on them," Starbuck answered.

"Down here!"

Jim Kane's summons rode above the noise of the fire. Shawn wheeled, threw his attention to that end of the canyon. Just outside its entrance he could see horses milling about. Some appeared to be carrying riders, others were not.

Valdez was going to rush them again. Once more he wondered at the Comanchero chief's impatience; it could be a matter of pride, he supposed, or possibly he was aware of something not apparent to the men trapped in the camp. But it was no time for conjecture; their chances of stopping the outlaws a second time were very small.

"Everybody!" he shouted. "Move up — toward Kane."

Lunging from the protection of the rocks, Starbuck whipped out his pistol, began to zigzag a course for the barricade occupied by Kane. The others, taking their cue from him, followed instantly, and soon had gained the bulwarks in the upper end of the canyon.

There had been only a scattering of gunshots. Catching his wind, Starbuck glanced back to the others.

"Everybody make it?"

Mayo, in with Adam Finch, shouted, "All right, here!" They had pushed the body of the dead guard aside. It lay against the base of the barricade.

Dagget, occupying the shelter vacated by Starbuck, was a bit slower in responding. "Got myself nicked some. Nothing bad — and I reckon I owe them a little blood. They getting set to charge?"

Shawn returned his attention to the confusion beyond the bodies of the horses killed in the first assault. There were at least a dozen mounts crowded into the opening, and what riders he could see appeared to be awaiting a signal — probably from Valdez.

Up on the rim the outlaws continued to fire, but the shooting was irregular and came from well-spaced intervals. It could only mean the Comanchero leader was sending most of his following to participate in the rush.

"Reckon this could be it," Kane said in his dry, blunt way, as he checked the magazines of the two rifles he was placing in readiness before him.

"One thing in our favor," Starbuck said,

looking to his own weapons. "They've got to come over those dead horses. Going to slow them down plenty."

"Enough — maybe," Kane murmured.

"How's your ammunition?"

"Getting down to bottom. Maybe another twenty rounds after this loading-up."

"Expect everybody's getting low. We make it through this —"

"Here they come!" Adam Finch yelled.

20

A blast of gunfire broke out at the mouth of the canyon. Simultaneously, a dozen horses thundered into the opening, heads high, manes flying, eyes rolling wildly. The half-broken mustangs poured into view, slowed, began to swerve and mill as they encountered the bodies of the animals lying dead in their path.

The shooting increased, both from the rim and the entrance to the deep sink. Riders began to appear beyond the turmoil of dust as the Comancheros sought to press their advantage under cover of the confusion created by the loose horses.

"Time to go to work," Kane said, grinning, and leaning forward against the rocks, began to throw a steady stream of lead at the riders.

Finch and Mayo in the barricade across the way immediately opened up and Dagget also began to use his weapon. Shawn saw two of the outlaws go down as the wall of bullets greeted them, but others closed in quickly. There were at least a dozen Comancheros, perhaps more, attempting to force an entrance behind the unruly mustangs, and their bullets, abetted by those of the outlaws Valdez had kept on the rim, drummed like a hail storm.

Abruptly the horses broke free, plunging out of the trap formed by the dead animals in front of them, the yelling, shooting Comancheros to their rear. One made a high, soaring leap over the stiffened shape pressing against his hooves. It set a pattern for all those behind him and suddenly the smoke and dust-filled air was filled with horses arcing over their prone counterparts.

"Look out!" Starbuck yelled.

The lead animals had cleared their initial obstacle. Now, at full speed, they were blindly racing straight at the barricade, seemingly unaware of its presence.

The long head of a horse, nostrils flaring, eyes rolling whitely in panic, neck outstretched, was abruptly before Shawn. As he shouted again at Kane, the animal left the ground in another frantic leap to clear the shelter. Starbuck reeled as a flailing hoof caught him a glancing blow on the side of the head. He fell back, taking a second blow as his skull came hard against the rock forming one side of the bulwark.

He lay motionless, stunned but not lost to consciousness, vaguely aware of the hammer of guns, the thud of hooves, the swirling dust and smoke, and the dim shapes of horses sailing by above him.

Starbuck shook himself angrily, pulled himself upright. To his left, Kane still crouched, rifle at his shoulder, as he aimed and triggered his weapon with cool, methodic deliberation. There was a hard smile on his lips and the sheen of sweat now glossed his face.

Again shaking his head to clear it, Shawn laid his rifle across the forward edge of the barricade and began to empty it at the Comancheros. It was difficult to find a good target in the blinding tan and gray pall. The outlaws inside the canyon now, thanks to the mustangs they'd driven ahead of them, were whipping back and forth, firing point blank at the shelters, hopeful of getting a bullet past the logs and rocks and bringing down a defender.

He'd been dazed for only seconds, Shawn reckoned, since there appeared to be as many outlaws wheeling about now as in the beginning. He heard Kane grind out a curse, swung his eyes to him. The gunman was mopping blood from his face with the back of a hand. A ricocheting bullet had opened a gash along one cheek.

Kane noticed Starbuck's close attention, winked, flung up his weapon, and resumed firing. They were having little better luck than the outlaws, Shawn realized. The Comancheros were constantly moving, weaving in and out, making good use of the screen of dust and smoke while those who had been unsaddled were crouching behind their fallen animals.

From above, the men on the lip of the canyon were continuing their attack, thus keeping the Texans in the barricades from exposing themselves in a search for better accuracy.

Pausing to reload hastily, Starbuck, glancing to the side, saw Adam Finch standing upright. The stableman had turned about, was facing the lower end of the canyon. He saw at once what had drawn Finch's attention.

The outlaws, taking advantage of the fact that all of the posse members were gathered at the mouth of the canyon, were climbing down the ropes that had earlier been thrown over the edge of the wall. Several were already on the ground and moving in. Starbuck's jaw hardened; he and the others would be caught in a deadly crossfire.

Weapon loaded, he began to add his fire to that of Finch. The man was still upright, legs spread, head thrown forward as he levered and fired his rifle at the approaching Comancheros. Two were sprawling in the dust. A third stumbled and fell.

Shawn saw Finch jolt as a bullet smashed into him, stagger as another drove into his body, but he stayed on his feet. Starbuck leveled at the nearest of the outlaws, dropped him in mid-stride, snapped a shot at another who spun half around, fell. He glanced at the ropes. They were dangling, empty; the last of the group daring to descend them was running for the rocks beyond the stockade. Shawn's bullet knocked him into the dry brush.

Brushing at the sweat and dust covering his face and misting his eyes, Starbuck turned to Finch. The stable-owner was on his knees, was slowly sinking forward.

"Guess I been called. . . ."

Starbuck pivoted at the barely audible words. Jim Kane had settled back, shoulders slack against the rock behind him, hands pressed to a dark stain spreading across his chest.

"Hope . . . you . . . find your . . . brother," he mumbled, his voice all but overpowered by the seemingly increasing gunfire, and toppled to one side.

Starbuck swore grimly. That Davey Joe would have found his repeat of the Alamo, were he there, was becoming evident now. There appeared to be no end to the number of Comancheros, judging from the thickening dust and the milling about at the mouth of the canyon — and the posse was down to John Mayo, Dagget, and himself.

He wasn't even certain of them. Earlier he had noticed the old lawman crouched alongside the barricade occupied by himself and Adam Finch, calmly firing into the surging ranks of the outlaws. He was not there now, could possibly have been hit and drawn himself back into the rocks. The pall was so dense he could not see Dagget.

Like as not they were dead, too — along with Jim Kane, Deke Benjamin, Finch, Willard, Davey Joe, Traxler, and Orvy Clark. And the odds were he'd not be long in joining them.

He'd failed in his efforts to reach Ben and free him from the outlaws, just as the long years he'd spent in search of him were now going for nothing. He could take satisfaction for only one thing; the Luddin wagon train. Those people would have made good their escape and —

A rider burst through the choking haze. Starbuck's arm came up, forty-five cocked and ready in his hand. He and the posse had made the Comancheros pay dearly for their efforts, and as far as he was concerned, it wasn't over yet.

Starbuck's finger tightened on the trigger. He hesitated; the man on the horse was wearing a bright red-and-blue uniform. Suddenly more soldiers rode into view and Shawn became conscious of a sudden decrease in the gunfire.

Across the way he heard John Mayo shout, saw the lawman step into the open, hand raised, palm forward, and move toward the soldiers. The officer in the lead whipped his mount sharply around, angled toward Mayo, now being joined by Mort Dagget.

Starbuck heaved a deep sigh, got to his feet. At least three of the original posse were getting out of it alive. He threw a glance to the rim of the canyon beyond the charred remains of the wagons. That was where he'd last seen Ben; he could be there yet, but the dense cloud of dust and smoke shut off the area from him.

Leaving the barricade, Shawn crossed to where Mayo and Dagget were facing the Federalista officer and several of his men. Over in the mouth of the canyon, other soldiers were herding Comancheros into a pocket in the rocks and setting up a guard around them.

"Was just telling Captain Rodriguez here that we're powerful glad he showed up when he did," Mayo said, turning to Starbuck. "He heard the shooting, figured it was Valdez and his bunch. . . . Told him how we tied them up, too, so's them wagon-train folks could make it back to the border."

Shawn nodded. The marshal, despite his recklessly exposing himself, was untouched; Dagget had a bloody arm where a bullet had tagged him.

"You hurt any?" the lawman asked. He noticed the crust alongside Shawn's head where the horse's hoof had grazed him.

"Only a scratch," he said, and shifted his glance to Rodriguez, thoughts of Ben again uppermost in his mind.

"The camp up above," he said, pointing to the end of the canyon, "my brother was there — a prisoner. Was he among the men you captured?"

Rodriguez was a lean, dark-faced man with a small, neatly trimmed moustache and hard, bright eyes. He frowned, stroked the hair on his upper lip with a thumb and forefinger.

"They had fled when we arrived, senor,"

211

he said in precise English. "Only those outlaws here in the canyon remained. It is likely they saw us coming and so departed. It was a brother this Valdez had made a prisoner of, you say?"

Shawn, weariness settling through him, nodded. Ben was either lying dead in the outlaw camp on the rim or had been taken by the Comancheros when they rode off after sighting the oncoming soldiers.

"Is it possible he was slain by the outlaws? There were several bodies —"

"Just saw him for a couple of minutes. They had his hands tied and a rope around his neck."

Rodriguez turned to a junior officer, said something in quick Spanish. At once the younger man wheeled, barked out several names and then, as a squad, all spurred toward the entrance to the canyon.

"I have sent Lieutenant Ortiz to make an examination of the bodies. He will return with word as to whether there is an American among them."

"Obliged to you," Starbuck said. It had been his intention to get his horse immediately and make the investigation himself. Rodriguez was having it done for him.

The prisoners who had been in the stockade marched by, surrounded by several soldiers, on the way to join the other out-laws. Rodriguez watched them pass, let his eyes drift on over the rest of the area. Most of the dust and smoke had lifted, and the extent of the fighting and its results were now more apparent. He nodded to Mayo.

"My government owes much thanks to you, senor," he said. "To lead so brave a band of men in here, and accomplish what you have, shows great ability and clever planning. You are to be commended."

Mayo's head bowed slightly. "Thank you, Captain."

Dagget, an angry frown suddenly pulling at his features, glanced at Starbuck. Shawn shook his head. Let John Mayo take the credit. The old lawman would be returning to live among his friends in Sabine Springs and the glory would sustain him for the rest of his life. For himself he had no need for it; the chances were he'd never pass that way again.

"It is likely, because of what you have done in the interest of ridding my country of outlaws, my government will overlook the matter of trespass by armed men. However, senor —"

"I am also a captain," Mayo cut in stiffly, "and your government sure as hell should. I only done what I had to. Countrymen of yours came across the border into Texas, which was trespassing too, and made prisoners of Americans. I had a right and a duty to go after them."

"True, but, as I say, it is a matter for my government to decide. Therefore, it will be necessary to conduct you and your men to my headquarters where —"

"Like hell you will," Mayo said in a flat, unyielding voice. "You'll have to shoot us first — in the back, while we're riding out —"

He broke off as Ortiz and the squad he'd taken with him pounded up and drew to a halt. The young officer reported quickly, saluted. Rodriguez faced Starbuck.

"Your brother was not among the dead. I fear he is still a prisoner of Valdez and those who escaped with him."

Relief moved through Starbuck. Ben was still alive — a prisoner of outlaws, but still alive. He looked up at the Mexican officer.

"I'm going after him, Captain."

Rodriguez' mouth tightened. "Such cannot be permitted, senor."

"Permitted or not, that's what I'm doing," Starbuck said coldly. "If you're going to stop me, you'd better begin now."

Shawn pivoted, started toward the corral where the sorrel had been picketed. Behind him he heard Rodriguez bark an order.

"Teniente, you will seize that man!"

Starbuck paused, tension lifting within him. John Mayo's voice reached him as he came back around.

"Let him go, Captain — be no harm in it, and he'll be helping you if he finds that bunch. . . . I'll make you a bargain. Leave him be, and me and my friend Dagget here'll go with you to your headquarters without any arguing."

Rodriguez considered Starbuck thoughtfully. After a moment he nodded.

"It is agreeable," he said. "You may accompany Lieutenant Ortiz, who will be going in pursuit of Valdez within the hour. You will place yourself under his orders. Such is clear to you?"

Starbuck shrugged. He would prefer to go alone; not only would he be able to travel faster, but the passage of a single rider would be far less noticeable than that of a company of soldiers. First things first, however; he'd take it as it came — change could come later.

"Obliged to you, Captain," he said, and let his eyes move on to Mayo and Mort Dagget. "Goes double where you're concerned."

The lawman bobbed crisply. Dagget

grinned, made an offhand gesture. Rodriguez gathered up his reins.

"I shall rejoin you and Lieutenant Ortiz within a few days," he said, wheeling about, and then leaning forward slightly he smiled down at Starbuck. "Adios, macho. Bueno suerte."

"Adios, amigo," Starbuck replied, and turned again to get the sorrel.

ABOUT THE AUTHOR

Ray Hogan was born in Missouri in 1918. Married, with two children, he has lived most of his life in New Mexico. His father was an early Western marshal and lawman, and Hogan himself has spent a lifetime researching the West. In the last 30 years he has written over 50 books, the majority dealing with the American West. His work has been filmed, televised, and translated into 6 languages.

We hope you have enjoyed this Large Print book. Other Thorndike, Wheeler, and Chivers Press Large Print books are available at your library or directly from the publishers.

For information about current and upcoming titles, please call or write, without obligation, to:

Publisher
Thorndike Press
295 Kennedy Memorial Drive
Waterville, ME 04901
Tel. (800) 223-1244

or visit our Web site at:

www.gale.com/thorndike
www.gale.com/wheeler

OR

Chivers Large Print
published by BBC Audiobooks Ltd
St James House, The Square
Lower Bristol Road
Bath BA2 3SB
England
Tel. +44(0) 800 136919
email: bbcaudiobooks@bbc.co.uk
www.bbcaudiobooks.co.uk

All our Large Print titles are designed for easy reading, and all our books are made to last.